SODOM AND A GREEK

PASSION

SUBTITLE

RAGS AND OLD IRON

Sodom and a Greek Passion

Subtitled

Rags and Old Iron

By
Robert Waltz

Cover Design by Marina
 415 305 1071
<waterdance@telocity.com>
Photo by Rob W. Waltz
Layout by <kim@bigwhitecat.com>
© Robert Waltz

All rights reserved. No part of this book may be reproduced without written permission from the publisher..

Canadian Cataloging in Publication Data

Waltz, Robert D. 1920-
Sodom And A Greek Passion

ISBN 1-55212-358-8
Fitst Printing 2000
Second Printing 2001

1. Title.
PS8595.A628S62 2000 C813'.6   C00-9103-340-6
PR9199.3.W3548S62 2000

COSMOS PRESS

San Francisco Bay
3426 Fleetwood Drive
El Sobrante, CA, USA

Sr. Editor, J. Francis
cell: 415 378 3923

CANADA SALES

False Creek, Vancouver
1150-f - Forge Walk
Vancouver, BC, Canada:

Author, R. Waltz - email
robertwaltz@hotmail.com

THE QUALITY OF WRITING....
in Robert Waltz's first book of his trilogy.
Sodom and a Greek Passion, is reminiscent
of the great Chicago and mid-western writers
who, looking back on the circumstances that
shaped their lifes, have produced memorable and
highly readable novels of lasting quality.
John Cross, Archivist. Jericho Literary Center

MR. WALTZ HAS A UNIQUE UNDERSTANDING OF THE HUMAN SPIRIT, replete with all its pathos and charm. He holds nothing back in his interpretation of a man's search for meaningful love. This is not a book to be read lightly. Be prepared for his stark, almost brutal honesty and his vivid power of imagination. You will come away changed.
Kim Hood, Author, Squamish BC, Canada

This latest novel by Robert Waltz brings to mind a review I wrote when publishing Waltz's second book, The Beaten and the Hungry. The same "fine, artistic writing, character and pace" is created here like in his early work, but with the added spice of a wonderously vital spirit that has aged well with this major senior writer.
edited review from PD Press, Prof. Dale Kolby, Atlanta, Georgia.

I enjoyed reading your novel very much. Perhaps my interpretation may be different from most people. For me it confirmed what I have always believed, "as human beings we have an incredible capacity to love." There is alot of humour in your novel which as an aspiring comedian I truly apprciate. Your book was refreshing and captured the reality of life. So many of us go through life pretending.
Lesa, Calgary, Alberta

BY THE SAME AUTHOR

fiction novels
Abandon
Olympia Press, Paris

The Beaten and the Hungry
Othello Books./Olympia Press, Paris - lst edition
Olympia Press, Paris, (hard cover) - 2nd edition
Pendulum Books, USA

translations
The Beaten And The Hungry
Dutch, Elsevier, Amsterdam
French, J.P. Bier, Brussels
Hebrew, Isklai, Atid, Tel Aviv
Over de Brug, *Elsevier Amsterdam*
Tara's Shadow, *Elsevier Weekblad*

short stories
Excised from Genesis
Tara's Shadow *Elsevier Weekblad*
Trade of the Spirit
A Bedewi Event
Kief
Plaka
Delphi
Love's Shadow Clouds Acropolis

The author is thankful to his first publisher, the late Mourice Girodias, who paid authors monthly, in Francs, Lire, Marks and Dollars, which kept writers fed in the memorable post-war years when Paris lured us to share its wonderfully uninhibited morals.

Acknowledgments

In four-score years an author has cherished tons of gratitude that would need half a volume to acknowledge — so I must limit my thanks to close companions for their support and encouragement during the writing of *Sodom and a Greek Passion* that has dominated my waking hours and haunted my sleep.

Syd and Anita Butler
Lorna Gentry
Jaqueline Mayer
Dianne Kennedy
Patrick Ng
Doug Taylor
Ken Wood
Marina, Ted
and Rob Waltz

For
Shoshanna and Rosemary
Their dark eyes forever closed beneath earth's crust
and
Barbara
Lost somewhere in love's world

and our children

**Chicago: Millicent Anne, Laura, Roberta
Rubin, Faye.
Vancouver: Robert William
El Sobrante, Francis Jules
Australia: Simon David William**

"Be self-satisfied, and other self-satisfied people will love you, rend your neighbor, the other neighbor will laugh. But if you hurt your own soul, all other souls will cry out."
Les Mots
Jean Paul Sartre

The scenes and episodes described in this tale are fictitious embellishments of events and locales, and the representations of characters to fallible humans, alive or not (including the author) is coincidental.

The Cabin

When a woman gets the blues,
Lord,
She bows her head and cries
But when a man gets the blues,
Damn
He borrows a buck and rides.

When a judge during prohibition in Chicago asked my Uncle Alfred, charged for being drunk and disorderly, where he left his wife and kids, my uncle answered by lying, "I got no family nowhere."

The judge figured that my uncle was a man who had suffered women. Sighing, the judge said: "I have to sentence you to sixty or ninety days in County Jail, one or the two, which do you want?"

Chicago streets were cold that winter. Uncle Alfred

took the ninety.

His wife Rose was my father's sister, a consumptive with twin girls. When Uncle Alfred got out of jail in spring the following year he used Rose lustily. She suffered a miscarriage the same month she was due in the TB Sanatorium.

I was a favorite of Aunt Rose who treated me to cookies when my sisters were not around and cried a lot while holding me on her lap. I last saw her thin face pretty with undertaker's makeup drained of suffering, her yellow hair framed with red flowers crowding the cushions of her casket. Rose was only thirty-three. The twins were a month short of six years old. Uncle Alfred took them to New Albany, Indiana, where Rosie and my dad were born. He left them there and came back to Chicago.

One image of my grandfather stays with me. A neat man with a yellow goatee poised under a dim light bulb in the doorway of his alley shack saying a polite farewell, radiating a sense of optimism despite that the country he got wounded for in the Great War was starving him.

He left us his wood cottage with a screen porch fifty miles northwest of Chicago on the shore of Fox River. There the kinfolk quarrelled and women got pregnant. There my grandfather went to sleep and died. My mother did not cry, but my father did.

Even during the Depression my folks would not sell Grandpa's cottage. Mom and Dad figured it would be my place for refuge when I went wrong in life. They kinda knew I would. Dad taught me boxing to defend myself on Chicago's mean streets. He encouraged me to feel the land and the river so that I could nurture on nature and not endure some cold room hidden in our rough city.

The roots of my street skills were toughened on Chicago's West Side. Youth cut different scars of memory: the nagging depression, school yard fights, hill-billy bandits called the 42 gang robbing the bookie joints, Mafia gunmen killing them in revenge.

I was a scrappy ten-year old kid adept at grabbing apples from bushel baskets on the sidewalk and out-running the clerks who chased me. Coal was our money-maker. With my kid gang we would hop onto moving coal cars and heave big lumps over the side to gather up and sell for ten cents a bushel basket. Our territory was between Madison Street and Jackson Avenue. North of Madison Street, the coloured kids did the same. South of Jackson were the young Italians. We dared not infringe on either domain.

If one of our own got into a fight and picked up a stick or a rock, we would take it from him and tell both guys that they gotta fight fair or don't fight.

One Sunday when I got to the tracks to meet for coal-stealing my friends were bounding down the embankment and yelling at me to get going. A big coal chunk tossed over the Madison Street viaduct killed a woman pushing her baby buggy. It took but one day for the police to round up us coal-stealers. They came at night to tell my dad to bring me to the Warren Avenue Precinct Station the next morning.

It was the same cop station where we would climb the window bars and swipe the bread and baloney from the window box stored there for the prisoners in holding cells on the second floor. I told the fat cop sergeant who took me in a room to question me that I wouldn't tell who threw that coal chunk over even if I knew. He boxed my ears then. "You little son-of-a-bitch, I think you do know. A white woman got killed, not a nigger."

His racist curse was the norm among the Irish and Anglo-American cops in the force of Chicago's police. I don't recall ever seeing a colored policeman driving a cop car.
That night was the first I would spend in a juvenile detention cell before the cops believed I was not there that morning when the woman got killed.

I saw my first murdered man before I was thirteen. He was shot by the school store on Waveland Avenue near LeMoyne grammar school. My dog licked bloody gore from the dead man's blasted face. I loaned a cop my penknife to dig out lead slugs from the window frame.

Whatever the sink of our poverty, I was not thwarted because of want. I did not know what to want. The neighbors I remember were on charity like us receiving sacks of raw oatmeal, cracked wheat, powdered milk, pecks of potatoes, and half a ton of coal each month. When we ran short of food we borrowed from Ella Mae's family down the porch from us. When they were short we loaned what we could spare. I liked Ella Mae, a skinny nine year-old girl whose brother would lift her dress so we could see the hairless slit between her thighs.

Edison Electric cut our electricity when we could not pay the bill. There were gas fixtures that still worked in the old tenements along West Madison. We lit them to light and warm our flat.

Every other block from the Loop downtown to Western

Avenue had a storefront church. My mother would take me and my two sisters to the Chicago Gospel Tabernacle run by big Mother Love from Arkansas. Up front were white-robed holy-rollers singing out their religion with angelic voices while writhing on the dusty stage till they wet their pants. We laughed at my mother doing that with them. Mom never slept in the same room with my father. Until I was twelve I had to sleep with my mother in her bed.

My dad, marked by boxing for two bucks a round in local clubs, was a man of frustrated gifts tolerant and patient. In middle age his guts were ruined from guzzling home-made wine and bootleg whisky. The Depression and putting up with my holy-roller mother drove him to boozing.

Fathers of my school-gang friends declined through despair into drinking until they were unemployable — examples of millions whose energy was dissipated, lost in the country's wasteland of sick enterprise which during the thirties could not profit from their flesh and so rejected them.

Horse-drawn wagons carried ice and coal through the back alleys. Once a week the junk man came, the foreign driver crying, "Rags and old iron, rags and old iron." I never saw a Colored man driving a junk wagon.

Westsiders were ignorant about others in the city and could only vaguely empathize with those Bronzeville Negroes on the south side living in conditions no less appalling than ours.

Poor Americans did not know how distorted and hurtful a nightmare the Depression really was, how many Americans lived on hope, believing that the government would do something. They trusted and were cheated by the profit nexus that they could not know was not designed for their well being. Chicago was a very big city to me and nothing was simple then. Like most American boys my heart harbored instincts of decency. and trust. But before escaping my puberty those instinct were frayed and I began to dedicate myself to the pursuit of sweet foods, adventure and sexual discovery. Laps of moonlight licked the bushes in Waveland Park when I lay with Rosemary, the first virgin to let me penetrate her, the first girl to bear me a love child, the first love-woman I would abandon..

    I was doing two months in the city juvenile detention home when my father was killed in a saloon brawl. My mother made the mad house the next winter. She froze to death in the asylum yard on a night when it was too cold for the staff to bother searching when they saw her empty bed.

    These memories from the past vex the soul, the way deserted children haunt a wayward father.

*   *   *

    When did all this happen? Here I am almost forty with a motherless infant son asleep in the back room of my granddaddy's old cabin on the Fox River. It is early spring now. The wind is fresh with thin rain. My chimney fire warms the cabin against the twilight chill splaying over the water.

    In a corner of the front room with the fireplace is an apple crate stuffed with books. Pressed between the pages of a torn bible is a blue envelope that I have never opened. The address, Box 1063, Sodom, Israel, was the field office of the Spoon River Construction Corporation at the Dead Sea where I was working when my son was conceived. The red express sticker in Arabic and Hebrew clings to the envelope like a cast mark over my name. It took five days to reach me from Jerusalem. Gideon's patrols, two thousand years earlier, marched the distance in two days.

The unopened letter was mailed by Avigdor Gudenov, whose wife Sarai was the dearest woman I ever cheated with. I did not open her husband's letter then, nor will I open it now for I could not tolerate that recollection and Avigdor's Hebrew spirit among the ghosts that already crowd me here.

Probing the human shell, groping through the rubbish of memory, searching for something palatable to digest is galling and self-infectious.

Although this Illinois valley is a long way from the Holy Valley of Siddim where Gomorrah and Sodom thrived in that scorpion sink of earth's waste, I cannot rid my body of its salt nor my mind of the tricky events that drove me from Israell to refuge in this river cabin.

Seven of the letters mailed to me here during the past winter were from Sarai. What she wrote was always sad. They described the mental tilt of her husband. In their troubled land of Israel he was more damaged in his psyche than Sarai. Through loving Sarai I loved her husband too. His Hebrew soul had withered. He was left with brittle senses like slivers of broken crystal.

Three other letters were from Nancy Carter writing to me from Greece. I had to control urges to fling Nancy's letters into the fire. I have not replied to her since returning here. What caused our parting will always color the memory of her expressive face beatific with tears, like the puzzled face of a choir boy blessedly used by his priest.

Nancy was fragile like a wren. Sometimes over the

river at dawn I imagine her shadow winging down from a low cloud, a tiny villainess feeding from plants with sparse nourishment, she nests, lays her sorrow, then slowly drifts away.

I asked Nancy once what the word love meant to her. She looked at me warily as if I had asked a cunning question, then answerd blandly, "It's an act, it's fucking. It's what we do, that's all it is — an act."

Sarai's letters I never failed to answer.

When I was with Sarai and Avigdor in Israel I tolerated her husband's madness, his suspicions about his wife, accusing her of every form of depravity — depravity which indeed Sarai performed with me after scheming to get him drunk so that we could get at each other. We were once together in Beersheba drinking tea after we made love: "How disgusting I must seem to you with my sensual obscenity. I am smothered by this surrounding Jewish orthodoxy for a god whose name we dare not write, Jawa, Jethro, Jehovah, Jesus. Why not call him phallus, it's what we mortals truly worship? Despite the holy stuffing fed me from the Gemara I cannot respect the simple commandment to be faithful to my husband who loves me, and our sons who love us. Oh Simon, if only I could cast off my Semitic skin and become a Christian or a whore."

Oh, unholy Sarai! How I need you now.

Her letter that came this week contains barbs of fear, *Ein Karim is still bizarre like when you were here. Each month more hippies come (Goyim and Jewishgirls) to occupy old Arab houses. There is a small damaged vacant house near our street. When I walk by it I imagine that you are there. But it is your friend from Athens who stays there now, Donald, the dark man you said was like a soul brother for you and Avigdor in Greece. He came looking for you. I try to take comfort from his brown body. What am I not ready to do to find peace. In the same letter she proposed putting her sons in a kibbutz and come here to me, then added, why not come back to Israel with your son? It would be good to have you in Ein Karim with us and your friend. Avigdor loves and trusts you which is quite unusual for him. He loves Donald also. I think they like each other like* Greeks, *but I am not sure. I wonder if I care? Did you three men do each other in Athens the way you and me did with each other?*

Damn the preternatural sexuality in women who dread torment. Anxious, loving Sarai, temptress Lilith. No woman, I will not return to your holy land to wallow in sin with you. I cannot suffer Avigdor's decay. Your husband's soul has been withering since Abraham cracked the sanction sacrificing the first born girl-child whose bones decay under the door stone of a million Hebrew years. The barbs of fear that pricked me were Sarai writing about Avigdor and Donald dealing with the *brothers*. Brothers was our code name for the Palestine Arabs. Avigdor, Donald and Yiannis were trafficking with the PLO according to this in her letter:

Avigdor and Donald went to Haifa and came back with Yiannis the Greek sailor who knew you and Nancy in Athens. They are dealing with the rebel Palestinians. They plot with them to smuggle something through Lebanon. I hope it is not guns. Dangerous and bad — very bad. There is fighting there. "Remember what you did before the government put you out of Israel? What they risk is much worse. I am afraid they will be killed. What should I do? Come to Israel soon. I need you. Please answer me quickly. It is a happy hour when I read your letters. Your words roll like pearls on my skin. David and Simon ask about your son, Francis-Guillaume (I like his name) does he have your blue eyes or her dark ones? I wonder if I should tell what my Simon said? He has been sneaking bottles of cognac to his father. When I asked him why, he said that his father looks crazy sometimes, and that if a doctor puts him in a crazy place you will return to us. Oh Moses what have we done to our men?"

Yes Sarai, what have you done to us? When I stare at my dark window I see a stranger with the vacant expression of a lost father. My spirit is like mercury in a time tube tilting memories between love and perfidy on this hectare of hell that men call earth. I know where soiled beds were shared, a trusting heart rended, a tender soul torn when a woman woke in the morning to find me gone. How can this be judged? A mans love is ordained. Name it lust and share it gently.

Athens, Beersheba, Jerusalem; Sarai, Nancy, Yael -- oh why recount the ancient sites and crying spirits? I cannot manage thoughts in an insensitive state. Fugitive memories cave in like character faults exposing dank dungeons where men hide their fears. Why in memory does everything conjure up the terrors in recollection? Checking that my son was asleep and covered I go out to the dark woods, frustrated from the past I damaged. I wanted Sarai touching me like she did when Avigdor lay alongside us in a drunken stupor. Her need was tender with love, mine a frantic masturbation spitting out the bitterness. The pain of ejaculation stains her letter. Lying on a skelton of roots the brutal need whips my force. Only my son asleep in the cabin keeps me from begging the ghosts of night to prick me with sweet death, to close my heart and deny me ever again tormenting another woman.

Plaka

Greece gripped me with its gout-gnarled hand. Nothing in its twisted palm could have forecast how a wayward girl would affect me long after our Greek love drama. Thinking about Nancy grated like a jagged blade across my chest.

We met two winters ago in Plaka, a haphazardly built quarter on the back slope of Acropolis Hill. I lived in a rooftop shack over a Greek merchant's house in the Plaka quarter of Athens. Entry was up stone steps built over the outdoor latrine.

My space was like a harp in form, the narrow back wall dug into Acropolis rock. It held two chairs, a split table, one coffee pot, two dishes, a cracked mug and a kettle. Heating and cooking was from a kerosene camp stove. The bunk was made with planks stuck in niches four feet off the floor. My one window opened over Plaka roofs past Syntagma Square.

My existence in Greece was unburdened and quiet. Never did I doubt that Nancy and I would do well together. She walked into Taverna Diogenes late one night where I was drinking wine with Yiannis a Greek mariner whose uncle owned the place. Costa the waiter was whispering something in Greek to Yiannis before we noticed Nancy. Looking to where Costa nodded toward a young woman with long hair, Yiannis told me that she had asked Costa to bring her to our table. She preferred not eating alone among Greek men. "I know this America kid," Yiannis said while Costa led her to our table.

After Nancy Carter introduced herself and before we could offer her a drink, old Nikos a philosopher and poet left his table to join us. Yiannis claimed Nikos was his uncle too. I learned later that was not true. Nancy was a small young woman with fine chestnut hair flowing over frail shoulders. Her face was pleasing with wistful green eyes, a wide mouth and high cheeks and the skin of a country girl tinted like flower petals. Her smile was a radiant flash of clean crooked teeth, one of sweetness mixed with a hint of anxiety. Just seeing her thrilled me. Her speech was a pleasing Arkansas drawl with a poetic lilt transmitting her feelings that urged me to focus on every movement of her mouth. At once I wanted her. I was into the Greek narcissist mode, hungry to feed on beautiful sex. Like Greeks I was not troubled by gender fairness. Equality of love is improbable among Greek men and women. Their ancient practice accords only physical pleasures to women. The psychic part of men is better fed among their peers.

Into that scene came this Baptist Archangel worshiping the Greek mood and myth. There was something about Nancy, like a bird's fey grace, that made me curious and sympathetic. I determined to have her. We were not evenly matched. She appeared less a slut than I was, but something was showing through, something I mistook for naiveté. I gathered that she could be hurt easily. She was one of the sisterhood of outsiders shielding her private world within her soul as a cushion against male predators. Our liaison did not last three months.

I had seen Nancy walking about Plaka, even passed her once in a narrow passage near where I lived. It was with some surprise when the subject of her person became our table topic although we did not know her and she did not know us.

Nancy had a theory about going it alone away from home ties and morals. Her personality and attitude seeped out in small doses while I watched and listened to her. Yiannis ticked her off with some of his remarks: "Greek women would not dare live alone in a country where they have no relatives."

"Because," Nancy cut in sharply, "you Greek males restrict their sensual freedom, while spreading your male sense of superiority around like sheep droppings. Our American culture tolerates equality and freedom between the sexes. Freedom with men can be expressed with masculine practice if I choose. But some of you I would rather not be equal with you are so damn lousy." She smiled before reaching to take one of Yiannis' cigarettes. I could not determine if her remark was a barb at Yiannis or all of us. It seemed that she meant him.

Old Nikos quietly cut in: "The matter of sexuality is too perverse, the cause too odd for public debate," reaching over the table to lay his wrinkled fingers on her slim wrist. "I like that you speak out. You are noble like Aphrodite. Throughout our ancient life it is women who have moved us. Without you we could be Turks."

Yiannis interrupted Nikos to remind him that they had an engagement elsewhere. Their leaving pleased me. I wanted to be alone with this young woman..

Nikos came around the table to bid goodnight,

caressing Nancy's cheek. She turned her face to kiss the palm of his hand. Yiannis, trailing Nikos through the taverna, looked back, his red tongue wagging beneath his dark moustache.

"Pig," Nancy muttered.

We two sat quietly smiling at each other while nibbling goat cheese and sipping wine. Putting her glass down, her slim finger caressing the rim, she sighed, "We have promiscuity but no liberation."

"What does love mean to you?" I asked her.

Tilting her head, exhaling, Nancy did not hesitate; "I say thing when that word crops up. "Why do you men ask this question for chris' sake? It's an act, fucking, it's what we do. That's all it is - an act."

"But we need it so much. There is a flaw in our being with no love."

"We are not much nourished from it," she answered, quietly.

"Love is a gift, not an appetizer."

Nancy leaned back, her wonderful eyes focusing on my face, her tongue caressing the rim of her glass. "Is it a gift? Is there not always something to pay?"

"In terms of exchange between two people, yes there is a price," I began. " When it's sincere it roots out selfishness. Then it becomes fair barter. Love is kindness and caring, and...." She hushed me by pressing her finger tips on my lips.

"You know, Mac," I would like you for a friend, but please don't misuse our time talking about your concept of the love thing. It makes me feel empty."

Her closing off my nonsense was gently done. Taking her small hands in mine, I said, "For you lady long-hair I shut up."

A wan smile spread her lips. Winking she leaned forward, again placing slim fingers on my lips and then pressed them on her lips, a sign I took to mean we could be partners that night if I wanted her. "Stay in Plaka with me tonight."

Looking straight into my eyes, Nancy softly answered, "Let's go."

She had drunk more than I realized. I supported her through the lanes until we arrived at my place. Slim as a goat she was no weight to carry up the stone stairs and put in my bunk where she passed into sleep when her head touched the pillow. I put my two blankets over her, wrapped an old army coat around myself and huddled against her. Before falling asleep I was thinking, *'I'll have her in the morning.'*

It was early when I woke the next day. Nancy's soft hair was touching my cheek. Easing off the bunk I lit the spirit stove and put coffee grounds in hot water over the flame. Then I opened the window to pee into the chilly morning over my landlord's roof. The sun was crowding a low bank of clouds. The hills had layers of hoar frost. Closing the window, I waited while the coffee boiled, watching the sun creep over the city to spill onto Plaka houses where old women were opening their shutters and shaking out bed linen.

Straining the coffee and tasting the first cup, I turned when Nancy stirred. Leaning on one elbow looking down at me she asked, "What are you drinking?"

"Retsina?"

"You're not?"

"No, it's coffee. Want some?"

"Yes please." Squirming under the blankets her head

emerged at the bottom of the bunk facing me. Putting my coffee mug down I stepped over to take her head in my hands and kissed green eyes that were not entirely cleared of sleep.

"Good morning, strange man."

"Morning, strange girl. One sugar or two?"

"One please."

Putting a sugar cube in my cup and adding hot coffee I handed it to her. She pushed herself up, swinging around, bare legs over the bunk's edge. Then she noted with surprise that she had slept in her dress.

"Oh damn. Did I drink too much? Can't quite remember how I got here except a vague feeling of being carried. Why did you not undress me?"

"Never occurred to me. Besides you might have come to, screaming rape."

"You can't rape me, I would give it. But my dress is terrible. I have a noon meeting with someone. I'll have to go home and change."

"Take your dress off. I can hang it outdoors for the wind to shake out the wrinkles."

"Do you have you an iron?"

"No."

"All right, but first where is the WC? I don't have a gadget like yours to dangle out the window."

"It's outside under the stairs. Do you care if my landlord sees you?"

"No."

"Come, I'll lift you down. Put my boots on and hurry back. It's nippy this morning."

While she shuffled out I toasted hard bread over the

flame using the last of my butter and marmalade for her toast. Returning, Nancy pulled off her dress and watched me with an amused grin while I went through the window to clothespin it on a wire. I offered to drape a blanket over her bare shoulders. She said she was not cold. I saw her differently in daylight, her fine hair in disorder over her neck and shoulders, her small feet still tan from last summer's sun. I stood her up, unhooked her brassiere and hugged her satin breasts against my cold chest. I put her on the bunk, kissed her body and climbed up beside her. Her responses to my caresses were beautiful. I have never before been kissed with such feeling by a woman who was with me for the first time.

Nancy was one of that rare type whose sexual grace and qualities emerge with force on intimate contact. "What a lovely curve to your thing. Can I suck it?"

She brought me to heat adroitly, fingers and tongue enflaming my passion until she rode on me to orgasm. Finished, we hugged adoringly. Holding her I thought how simple it was to control the defects of being alone with a creature like Nancy with soft breasts and perfumed love cleft at her center.

"Cover me with all of you."

"There will be no getting out from under to make your appointment."

"I know."

We moved through one another the whole morning, then slept. The afternoon passed quickly. The sun had shifted far to the right of the window. Nancy, sitting up in the bunk kicked off the covers, clasped her ankles and looked at her new lover. When I pulled part of the blanket over my waist she took the corner between her fingers and folded it away to leave me exposed, then turned to look out the window.

Her ingenuous silhouette was framed in the bright sky. Watching her like a serpent fascinated by the unconscious grace of a small bird, my senses curled like fumes of opium. My soul was floating in space beyond ecstasy, guts tingling, chest smarting from her bites at climax that endowed our act with sacredness. Then from her mouth fell the petals of a song in clear alto, sweet and light as a eunuch's voice.

My surprise was sudden, causing my eyes to tear. My Aunt Rose could sing like that.

When leaving before twilight she said, "please don't ask where I live, or look for me. I will come back, trust me."

I hoped that it would not be long before she would return to Plaka. And I had doubts whether or not she would come back to me. A week would pass before we met again. During that time I savored the quality of our pleasure. There was no hint foreshadowing tension, no sense that love's demand could mar this union.

Wrapped up in her song was a mournful cry too weak to last beyond doubt. The love thing should be mad without heart or mind. She never named it other than thing.

During the next month of irregular mating Nancy abandoned herself to bazouki music in Plaka tavernas where the hungry come to feed on each other, where Greeks pressed ouzo and cognac on us to keep her among them longer. She danced like a Greek boy until I became annoyed and left the taverna. Before dawn she crept into my bunk unable to control her anguish until it spilled out in racking sobs. She submitted to Greek men like a victim — to me like a naughty child. I could not see beyond the cauldron of heat and steaming passion to the deeper personality that might explain her behavior.

Her memory still smarts, splashing like spilt wine over my body.

Schmuck that I was I mistook her pain for love.

Lincoln Lucas

My American friend in Plaka was Donald Lincoln Lucas, a forty-year-old, lighttoned Negro from Chicago whose round boyish face softened his age. He was a plump man with curled dark hair greying at the temples, hazel eyes, and a trim moustache. Among the Greeks he passed as the son of a North American Indian Chief, a ruse that easily worked.

Don and I were both Leos born five days apart in Chicago's Cook County Hospital. When we met in Athens our pursuit of happiness was not dissimilar — to function in a good space with whatever solitude and pleasure we could get at minimal moral cost. In the Plaka quarter on the backside of Acropolis Hill our simple pleasures were shared.

There was something about Donald's spiritual makeup that seemed far removed from the racist America he served, fought for and abandoned. A complex man of learning and culture Lucas could express himself with biblical and poetic phrases as well as blunt terms. He could be vulgar like a ghetto spade when angry. Donald was a likeable friend when he wanted to be liked, and a mean black man when aroused.

During that winter in Greece I learned how terribly his kinfolk had suffered in the South. And it was no doubt that suffering which sharpened his intuition and distilled the quality of volatile magic that he used to much advantage in his intercourse with people.

He was a clever commentator and critic of our foibles. When he was sober he was the most eloquent of our foreign clique in Athens. Even when he drank he never lost his aura of loneliness.

He was a barefoot farmer's kid when his family decided to send him to Uncle Partridge in Chicago to get educated. All through high school he was lead cantor at the Baptist Tabernacle on 39th and Drexel. Mahalia Jackson heard him and had him sing at her church where she broadcast Sunday mornings. From high school he entered the liberal Roosevelt College on Michigan and Van Buren. That was his first schooling where the student body was not all Colored, and where he established friendship with white guys who, to his surprise were mighty radical and genuinely unbiased against Negroes. It was there he formed a close relationship with several white radicals who encouraged his plan to liberate Chicago's poor Coloreds from white racist politics.

Donald L. Lucas, a decade later formed the fierce Urban Cuban Guerrillas who occupied a quarter of Chicago's south side to form an inner-city state.

I learned about that in small doses from him. In Ankara his foreign service abruptly ended after the ambassador's wife caught him tangled in a raunchy LSD threesome with her twin sixteen-year old daughters. The kids got that hushed up by threatening their mother with exposure for enjoying Donald more often than they had. Shortly after that, suspicions were whispered connecting him with the Chicago insurrection that occurred a decade earlier.

Underground people who work in government departments got word to Lucas that an order transferring him back to Washington was a ruse to get him on home soil where agents with the FBI wanted to ask some questions about his past activities. He had quietly left his posting and slipped into Greece with a different name and passport.

Don and I discovered that we knew people in common in Chicago and became close friends that winter. Neither of us intended our relationship to become as complex as it did.

I could not then delineate why I had come to Greece. It was a handy place for dreaming, suspended in a void between Chicago and the Middle East. Whenever I think of Greece, deep pools of reminiscence surge through me, stirring the anguish I still harbor about Nancy.

Little by little I learned why Lucas was living in Greece and a lot about his character. He was a man pummeled by shadows — shadows that partly faded when he was stoned on hashish or well gone with wine.

When he drank alone and I came upon him by chance, he was still mellow and kind. But if he drank in company and discussions turned into arguments, his temper rose. The frustration, suffering and anger at being a Negro in America, dominated and used by whites, spilled from him. However, despite what I was to learn about his violent participation in the Chicago Rebellion he never broke things, never threatened us personally.

I found him several times too drunk or doped to climb stone steps in Plaka to find his room. When the hash pipe and the bottle's numen led him into tempests of absurdity I would nurse him. It would take most of the night and part of the following day to bring him back to lucidity, waiting out his weeping and storming, his threats of mayhem to Bastard Whitey or damage to himself.

Recovering by twilight, his nature became tender. Comforting him like a lover calmed Donald and he would see to what rank his debauchery leveled him. He was intelligent enough not to settle for basal existence. He straightened out for a while, proudly showing me his translations of Greek poetry. He would freely interpret Greek classic poetry until it read differently in English. Then he would re-work the poetry back to Greek without referring to the original. The effect was magical.

Several hours in the Plaka steam house would cleanse us. There heavy Greeks loitered, spread obscenely on hot stones working up dark erections. Donald preferred not to visit alone. He knew which men at the baths were rough and aggressive until relieved with mutual masturbation. Because of them I usually accompanied Lucas. And because of them we found ourselves locked in one noon when normally everyone is turned out for lunch and siesta. Six men stayed in with two attendants who told Lucas what to expect.

"*Oike, oike,* (no, no)" he was replying with some annoyance. I understood that Lucas wanted no part of something.

I was still towelling my hot skin when the side door was unlatched and four schoolboys edged in who could not have been much above ten or eleven years of age. They were dressed in shorts and soiled sneakers. They dropped their clothing in a pile, exposing thin unwashed bodies. They were hungry slum kids driven to prostitution through ignorance and neglect. After more discussion between Lucas and the attendant he turned to me saying that we must go below, explaining that the kids could be hurt if we caused trouble. We need not use the kids, but we could not leave for fear we would tell the police and bring a raid on the place.

A dim corridor led to stone steps going down to the boiler room. It was so hot that we were sweating before entering a large cellar with mats laid over the floor. There everything took place, buggery. flagellation, oral sex.. Lucas motioned me to participate with the others. We both had erections. I shook my head and left mine alone. He did not. It was a curious experience that I had forgotten until now.

A Sunday Afternoon

Nancy came to Taverna Diogenes, our favorite Plaka taverna, on a Sunday afternoon when I was having a late lunch with Lucas. Studying Nancy's features after introduction, Donald asked in Greek if she was the dancer in a Piraeus Port cafe billed as La Petite Venus.

"Singer, but nobody in Plaka knows that. Can we keep it between us three?"

"You sure are a surprise close up," Lucas said to her. "One would never detect the pagan in your makeup, you look so country American close up."

Nancy simply looked at him.

"How does she appear in her act?" I asked Lucas.

"Like a Greek, which is how I am paid to seem like," said Nancy.

"More like a French tart," Lucas corrected.

"All right, so there I am French."

"Do you sing in French or English?"

"French and Greek."

"Like a Greek oriole," Lucas said, "but with a terrible Greek accent."

"Your colored pal?" Nancy asked me, raising her chin towards him, "two reflections against me in two minutes. Is he with you, against me, or what?"

"Knowing Don's fondness for orioles, I would think that in his peculiar way he is probably for you."

"Sorry," Lucas said without explaining.

When Costa brought her food she could not hold a fork with her left hand because of a swollen wrist.

"Have you fallen?"

"No," passing her knife to me.

"Injury?" Lucas asked, showing concern.

"A Greek," she replied.

"In your Piraeus cafe?"

"No."

"Only money or passion would cause a Greek to damage a woman."

Nancy looked straight into his eyes as though penetrating his bronze skull.

"Lucas, hold off please," I urged. "Nancy's private life is not our business."

"Sorry."

Sorry! That one word of courtesy Lucas carelessly uttered. did not come out like a serious apology.

Nancy did not hear it as an apology, if indeed she heard it at all. I knew it as a flake of his Don's protectibve crust to prevent Nancy probing into his dark soul where fairness and decency dwelt.

Conversation lagged while Nancy ate. Lucas was alert,

Sodom and a Greek Passion

expecting at least an insult or indifference from Nancy. Their postures were like those of a lizard and a scorpion wary of each other.

I regretted that Lucas was with me on Nancy's return to Plaka. She appeared troubled and harder in appearance than the week before. Taking up her glass she would grimace with her eyes closed appearing to blot out Don's presence. I felt that she wanted to relax, perhaps to rest with me without being grilled by a guy she had never met before.

Calling Costa to take away her neglected food Nancy asked him to bring a special wine from the cave, Cavalier de Rhodos.

Lucas asked where she had learned to speak Greek.

"On my own from books, here in Greece."

"Uh, uh," he doubted, shaking his head. "The expressions you use come from people quite native to this area."

Nancy shrugged.

Costa returned with two bottles, filled our glasses, then cleared the table of everything but square chunks of goat cheese. We finished the first bottle with sparse conversation.

Nancy did not smile much though I said things that should have pleased her. She gave the impression of listening to another dialogue, watching a scene other than ours with Greek men dancing in the taverna. The drift of her thoughts was silent. I felt uneasy for her.

The wine from Rhodos is full bodied and deep red coming from vines that sent the first plants to France two thousand years before. Lucas watched Nancy while she drank. I did too. When we met here the first time Nancy's drinking had governed her behavior in my room; carelessly drunk that night, recklessly sexual the morning after. That afternoon I wanted her sober.

Lucas' features seemed more tense than usual. He was observing Nancy with perception, some condescension, and not a little malice. Ordinarily with strangers he was a person of charm and simplicity. I could not detect why he would not conceal that he was viewing her from a point removed in sympathy.

Suddenly sitting erect, Nancy shook her head when Don tried to re-fill her glass and became a woman with assurance who never doubted herself in the company of men.

"Been to many islands?" I asked Nancy, to steer the talk to a casual level.

"Quite a few. I have a boat and often sail wherever the wind blows me. This winter my boat is in a work yard getting an overhaul with a longer bow sprit to attach a second jib. By spring I will have saved enough money from the cafe work to sail most of next summer; Crete, Rhodos, Cyprus, then perhaps Israel."

"Do you sail alone?"

"Generally, yes. I prefer being alone on the water. There are fewer frustrations anchoring off shore. Island Greeks won't leave me alone when I tie up at sea villages."

"I sail too," Lucas said. "You must be a good navigator."

"Fair," she replied, "taught myself with help from a local sailor."

"Not afraid to get lost?" I asked.

"Ever since Ulysses, men have lost their way in the

Aegean. Why should not a woman?"

Another facet to this fascinating girl I thought, picturing Nancy between rock islands at dawn, singing to the green water and bright sky. She noticed me studying her and smiled, than turned to Lucas, "What is your boat?"

"A fifteen meter, two-masted schooner. She is berthed in Turkey. I share ownership with two other men."

"Consular people?" I asked.

He gave me a sharp look to signal that I should not have brought up his connection with that service.

"Personal friends," looking at Nancy, " traders who use the Mediterranean for their commerce. We sail exclusively in Levant seas."

To evade further questions about his boat, Donald poured wine from the second bottle into Nancy's glass, surprising her with a question: "Have you plans for tonight?"

Gritting her teeth, lips apart, looking at me, then toward him, Nancy said, "I am in Plaka to be with this guy for several days of rest," placing her injured hand on my wrist.

"Come with us to a taverna across town? We're invited to the owner's name day celebration. He's expecting us."

"I am much too tired. But don't let me upset your plans." Turning to me: "If it's all right I would like to go to your room. When you return I should feel better and be good company. Right now I'm not thinking straight."

I had forgotten my promise to Lucas' friend about his name-saint celebration. I offered to pass it up. Nancy preferred I go. She moved her hand up my arm to caress my face, than winced because bending her wrist hurt. I gave her my key. She stood up, kissed my cheek, said goodnight to Donald without offering her hand, turned and walked slowly through the taverna, passing through the open door into the street without looking back.

"A minor Aphrodite," Lucas said when I turned from watching Nancy leave. He was completing an obscene Mediterranean gesture, fingers and thumbs joined, then extending the middle finger.

"Donald, ordinarily you charm people whom you meet. With this girl you cannot conceal a certain hostility. Why?"

The wine gone, he poured us some cognac, picked up his glass to sip from it while looking towards the empty doorway into the street. "A touch of humorous insight could save her from a lot of suffering."

"I didn't find how you spoke to her amusing."

"What did I say to bother her?"

"Your attitude bugged her more than your comments."

"Sorry, I wasn't aware I was drinking too much."

"The cause is more than drink, my friend."

"All right Mac, I'll tell you like I feel it. That kind of white chick bugs me. A new-world sex cat trying to play at being Greek. An American baby-doll whose happiness lies just beyond the cloud of her affliction, slipping into sexual whimsy to rationalize her conduct. It takes more than a night of Greeky sex to do anything for that species."

"Man, O man, you sure are hard on her. Mighty hard for a first judgment. What do you think she rationalizes? What affliction?"

"Wasp guilt, probably Baptist guilt. She has a Bible Belt drawl when she talks. Bet you a bottle of cognac you will learn that she ran out on mommy and daddy, and a host of guilts: sin guilt, racist guilt, feminine guilt."

"You have got a bet. Right off I cannot agree with you. Give me a month to know her better."

I thought his judgment of Nancy unwarraanted. To block any more unfavorable comments from him with her not there, I asked what he saw in Piraeus where she worked. "Have you seen her act at the cafe?"

"Twice."

"What does she do there?"

"Dances well, and she's a good singer. Her voice is real fine but Greek songs don't suit her. She sounds church trained. I bet she sings a mean gospel."

"She does. I have heard her sing. Is that all she does there?"

"In Piraeus night clubs, one either entertains or bends over."

"That kind of place?"

"For a hundred drachmas even the waiters can be had. Have you not been in the port clubs at night?"

"Nope, can't afford them."

"If Nancy cares for you she may not want you to see her at work with a tight navy blouse, leather panties and white boots, appealing to every sailor's kink."

"I doubt if it would matter if I saw her there or not. She projects what she is and a man can like it or not."

"Another feminine lib kid."

"Oh please, Don, let's not start on her again."

He lifted his open hand, pink palm forward making a circle movement with his arm, a gesture I was to see often when he was either trying to dismiss something from his mind or bring on something that was deeper than the subject.

"You know, Donald, I had not observed you around a woman before now. Do you have nothing generous to say about them?"

"I do not admire white women, and seldom a white man. I know damn few men like you who are not threatened by my brown skin. The weak men most women settle for have no appeal for me, no thoughts worth proving. Though you're a wasp you are not the Whitey we quarrel with. I don't see your color any more than you see mine."

"Thanks. A sweet statement that. I treasure the compliment."

"One you merit, Mac. You got the empathy of the rare northern liberal. Your intellectual processes tune the mind to urge humanity do the right thing. What a blessing all ethnics would enjoy if this were universal."

He closed his eyes and appeared to be praying, whispering yes, yes, then opened his eyes and drew a deep breath. "There is a gap," he began, "a gap which may be grotesquely wide, between what a man feels about himself and what he reveals under stress. The second is identified by the system haunting me and hating me, as I hate it. The first is personal and I'll dilate about it with you because I want you to know why I am who I am. And because I like and trust you I want to fill in the gap — the whole story, nothing held back."

Again he made the circle movement with open palm. "It's been choking my innards since I been here idle, hiding here with no meaningful work to keep my mind occupied, no challenge to sabotage whitey's institutions. What I mean is — well, damn it, I need a buddy to pour me on, and you're it.

There is averse hippies used to sing in my College club where I went most Sunday nights, two lines that I always remember: *"... he's my brother, he ain't heavy...."*

"I like that — brother, I'm your white soul brother.

"No, never mind the pigment, You, Simon William MacDonald and me, Donald Lincoln Lucas, soul brothers. That's what we are, soul brothers."

Saying this while he took my hand pleased me. Ever since meeting him I had wanted to turn on with Donald. He was too fascinating to let slip out of my life before I knew him better. He was the embodiment of the fatal rift in a culture where a man must be either a white man or a black man and not simply a man.

I knew something about the troubles a black citizen endures back home in America, but not much about Donald Lucas the man. A secret man who is a Negro does not get courted all over the states by liberals and deeper souls unless there is something to him. From his history alone I would guess what I saw in Donald: unusual character, a force of intellect, of drive, of sheer presence, and a softer nature of love that lies beneath the dark flesh of most Colored Christians.

Isolation in Plaka with other stragglers like me offered little scope to Lucas' intellect. Like my idle time, his was temporarily smothered waiting for what next life would offer up besides tight cunts, loose boots and a warm place to jerk-off.

Perhaps I had too much wine in me to ask Don how he knew my full name. Surely I never told him.

Sarai's Husband

Avigdor wrote to me from Jerusalem to ask if he would find welcome should he disembark in Piraeus on his way to Paris. He added that he would understand if I said that I could not accommodate him. Replying, I wrote that that he must come, sketching a detailed map to my Plaka door from Syntagma Square where the bus from the port would put him off.

He arrived one morning before eight o'clock. Nancy's head was on my shoulder. His knocking startled her.

"Ask who it is. Maybe it's immigration police."

"It's Avigdor, I recognize his voice."

Diffident, but excited, Avigdor made a good impression on Nancy. While we were having coffee, she said, "Your Israeli friend is handsome, I like him." Her remark made the day for Avigdor setting a good tone for his visit.

Nancy knew about my affection for his wife. It made her doubly sympathetic towards him. Avigdor was not good looking. His nose was neither Semitic nor Russian which was his ancestry. He had thinning light hair, a bulging Slavic forehead, deep furrows over dark eyebrows and a thin mouth. His features aged him beyond his thirty-four years.

    I had not told Nancy anything about Avigdor which might color my opinion of him. One of his father's cousins and his mother's brother were mad. An aunt suffered from fearing that she would again be taken to Treblinka from where she was rescued at the end of the war. On another level of eccentricity, Avigdor's brother had turned communist and was meeting secretly with a Palestine Liberation group. Two young cousins quit Judaism to become nuns in a Nazareth retreat famous for rearing fat white hogs.

    Avigdor sometimes exhibited behavior that was far off the wall of standards other men believe to be normal. Many facets of behavior marked my Israeli friend who had a lean body like mine and a ruder sexual attraction. He grinned more than he smiled, snickered or grunted rather than laughed aloud. His rare smile was infectious. When he was pleased his mouth made beautiful movements reciting poetic Hebrew and sometimes grandiose nonsense. When agitated his black eyes pierced through me.

    Coming upon Avigdor one morning sitting on the outer edge of the Acropolis looking eastward, he was a picture of desolation, his expression mournful as though something was burdening his soul. The heavy history of Judaism bent his shoulders. He once told me that the Jews' suffering was his fault. I feared for his sanity.

    Like most things emitting from a self-doubting man his fugitive reflections were mystifying. Lucas once summed him up succinctly: "Avigdor Gudinov is a madman who believes he is Avigdor Gudinov."

Avigdor was one of the few Jews I knew who drank heavily. We had similar feelings about many things: freedom, liberalism, and the folly of being governed. But his emotions simmered at a higher pressure. During his Plaka stay I watched his eyes that never ceased darting to all three of us as though gauging our reaction to anything he said. They dimmed when he drank, sinking away into near blindness when he would mutter..."my Russian families, we can't count them. My grandfather is always telling how we were taken by the hundred German trucks — I was hiding and counting them. We never came back."

"Not you Avigdor," Nancy said gently, touching his arm. "You mean that your grandfather hid and counted them, and you learned about that from your father, isn't that it?"

"Maybe like that," he agreed looking sadly at Nancy, then glancing toward me, and back to her as if they shared a private secret. Nancy and Avigdor's first encounter in my room did not explain why she took him away after breakfast. I did not see them again before that evening in Taverna Diogenes.

I had to forcibly restrain my curiosity. Sexual jealousy is the meanest of male emotions. Nothing helps much when one looks for illumination of suspicion, like Nancy lighting two cigarettes in her lips placing one in Avigdor's mouth, her fingers on his wrist while he spoke with her, filling his wine glass before mine.

I was connecting the scene with my own culpability and shame. Guilt from my knowledge of everything carnal, shame to question her right to behave as she wanted. And too, I was afraid that any demonstration by me would lose her. I loved them both, Nancy for herself and Avigdor through his wife

Sarai. If I had ceased to love or trust them my isolation would crush me.

It takes a little compromise to keep cool with jealousy present. I suspected but held my thoughts. My suspicions lasted all the time Avigdor was there. It proved a useless irritant. Sarai later told me that her husband had been impotent for years.

Many things contributed to my discomfort during Avigdor's visit, and to the disquiet his presence brought: Nancy's concern for him, his sensless drinking, his deportment when he was with us in the taverna. .

I would like to have remembered Avigdor and Lucas heroically like intelligent men professing incompatible philosophies in the light of logical argument. What I saw sometimes was petulant quibbling, expositions of impatience, self-projections, little empathy. They carried what the Greeks will not carry — uncertainty.

I fought against altering the view of these friends for whom I cared. I had always thought myself deeply concerned with the motives and passions of other people. Wherever I circulated in the sensual underworld of men and women using excitement and experience to trespass other bodies, sharing ignorance and poverty with them, I treasured my involvement with others, and sustained by this I remained civil.

But my civilized veneer began to thin. I was almost hollowed by their absurd sense of self-containment. The sediment of meanness stirred in me, rising to the surface forcing remarks I would rather have left unsaid in their company. My chagrin was sometimes taken out on Nancy.

On Avigdor's third night in Athens we were waiting for

Nancy in Taverna Diogenes. Lucas, Avigdor and I were eating and drinking too much. Avigdor was expansive, argumentative and comic. But in a moment he would change, drawing into himself to commune with some privy beyond our space.

Lucas displayed a desperate cleverness that marked the struggle of a dark American trying to emancipate himself from a fiery past into an easier present. Changeable, sometimes displaying his mercurial charm, or anger, or love, his haunting memories rose to trouble his mind.

Nancy's eyes were strange lights, sometimes flashing eagerly, other times dimmed with the pathetic hint of melancholy. Her presence warmly touched each of us. In no way imposing her force wittingly she was the catalyst for physical and intellectual rivalry among us three. Like most free American women she exuded an exotic love vibration that shares kinship with eternity. Nancy aimed every time at pure love and often believed that she had achieved it.

With her we formed a haphazard comradeship of outsiders carrying our private persons enclosed in fragile shells as defensive carapaces against the public world we could never hope to change.

Lucas and Avigdor had nearly consumed one copper pitcher of ouzo with hors d'ouvres while waiting for me. Nancy was the subject of their topic when I arrived.

Avigdor was saying: "For me Nancy is Aphrodite and Venus in one soul."

"You should see her seductive act at Cafe Venus.. You would add the strumpet Lilith to her list of credits," I told him.

"Watch it Mac," Lucas warned, smiling "Hebrew folklore has Lilith the first wife of Adam."

"A nice dodge, I replied. Who married them?" Avigdor did not get our play, his concern was on Nancy"s cafe character.

"After dinner, let's go to the port," Avigdor said turning to me as I sat down. "I might fly off soon and it would be a sweet memory to keep."

I shook my head. "Nancy is not up to working this weekend. She'll be here soon."

"Why? Is she with child?" Lucas asked.

"What?"

"Pregnant."

"No way, Christ, we don't need that."

"Losing your powers? You've been violating her for a month. She should be with child by now."

"Your attitude is peculiar tonight, even malefic."

"Because I joke?"

"Are you really joking, Donald?"

"Smoking," Avigdor cut in. "We dragged some hash earlier. Maybe it pricked Iago's envy."

Lucas was going to say something else to me but changed his mind, addressing Avigdor instead. "Were you not scheduled to fly off today, or is it tomorrow?"

"Yesterday. Changed my plans because I feel good with you guys and Nancy. I want to stay more. Athens is well alive after midnight, not dead like Jerusalem. When do Greeks sleep? I can't leave these pleasures yet."

"Tourist pleasures, or those peculiarly Greek?" I asked.

Packed with drink already, Avigdor sat back rolling his eyes upward and grimly smiled. "Levant joys you probably would not condone. Taking up a coffee jug, he poured some into three glasses, dropped sugar cubes in them and handed Don and me a glass. He sat back sipping his coffee, watching us with a curious smirk on his face.

Avigdor had picked up clues from me about Lucas' rebellious activities. Lucas himself had briefly hinted about his Chicago period when we had talked about it with Avigdor present.

"Donald," he asked, "your species are labeled terrorists in the Middle East, not revolutionaries. If it is not too disturbing tell me how you became the Simon Bolivar of Chicago?"

What do you know about a hero like Bolivar?"

"From early kibbutz textbooks that dealt with other heroes than Zionists. Simon is a good Hebrew name. Bolivar is not included in our Israeli schools however. His revolutionary ideas are too risky to expose to our Moshavim who camp between enemy Arabs and our coastal cities.

"Who are they?" I inquired

"Students training for military service while studying at the kibbutz where they live."

Lucas asked, "Are they the Black Jews I saw working the fields between Beersheba and Dimona?"

Avigdor nodded. "Refugees from Syria, or Morocco. The government settles North African Jews between the Arabs and our coast. They know the Arabs and speak Arabic."

"Hot damn! I knew I was right. I told them at the consulate but they said not."

"Told them what?"

"That your Israel is a black Jew's country."

"No, it's not."

I wondered how dark the sun goggles were that Lucas wore when he was in Israel.

"Your antecedents were all black," Lucas continued. "The wife to Moses was a sorcerer's daughter. Aetopian she was called, a woman blacker than you or me. All you Hebrews be high yella coloreds. You are Africans. Your ancestors like my ancestors were dark folks out of Africa."

If he believes that, I thought, it's unarguable.

Avigdor, picking out olives from a feta salad merely shrugged while Lucas continued,

"Your rabbis upset mother rule centuries ago. Greek and Hebrew myth had women on the level with Gods and Satan. Adam was described by the Greek term Andro-gyne, a bi-sexual like me. Rabbis later set him up as perfect, misled by impulse instead of by a temptress. Adam sampled each animal on earth but that was unsatisfying. He petitioned the preacher for something different. The Man upstairs fashioned a two-legger we call Eve with a gash for Adam to amuse himself with."

"You exaggerate," I said, amused and surprised by Lucas' vulgar folk vision. "Adam was stirred by the mysterious source of love, not conquest."

While Lucas was lecturing, Nancy appeared in the taverna doorway. Approaching slowly she held a finger to her lips for me to let her remain unnoticed by them.

"All this sex-myth scholarship is beyond me, but your fear of women is transparent," Avigdor said to Lucas.

"Moses, your guess just misses. My fear is unhappiness, not social failure like you peckerless whites. Nothing a man does can hurt me. A woman can damage more by what she witholds than by any spite she might display. Avigdor took a long time sipping his coffee before replying. "You know Donald, during the few days I have been here you have often surprised me. I had not imagined you aware of feminine cruelty."

From what I knew of him and his wife Sarai,, I wondered what level of cruelty Avigdor was referring to. .

Lucas nodded his head without comment. A big smile came on his face, then faded slowly as if unsure how to welcome Nancy whom he had just noticed.

She kissed me on the cheek while reaching over my shoulder to shake hands with Avigdor and Lucas, than walked around to take the vacant chair between them.

"*Kali spera — jasu,*" Lucas said, while offering her a glass of retsina.

"Nancy," Avigdor remarked, "in those white jeans you are a menace in this taverna."

"From what I overheard from you guys any female clothed in white would be a threat."

"Propitious, your entry at this point," Lucas said.

"Delicious," Avigdor smacked his lip and showed his tongue.

Lucas continued, "Your habits and appearance, your ideas are all evidence of what I've been saying. You epitomize the female desire for pristine rights."

"What do I want to revert to?"

"Top species on the pansy pole," Avigdor shrieked, bounding up to spin around the table like a dervish dancer.

"I may sing like a bird, even fly after drinking Greek cognac, but I'd rather perch on the penis than fly around the silly thing."

"I see we like the same symbols," Lucas said to her. "I must admit that I sometimes think of you as a young guy, particularly when you are candid about how you are."

"Take that as a compliment, Nancy," I said, reaching over the table to take her hand in mine.

"I can never be sure how to take what he says."

"Yes, do take it as a compliment. I see you as a Greek boy, and Greek boys are beautiful."

"All of this because of her slacks," remarked Avigdor, looking down at them and then up her body to look into her face, a wide smile spilling out his affection. "I drink you, American beauty," licking the rim of his glass.

"Slacks," said Lucas, "like sluts, use the tokas, like a Greek uses the tokas to attract."

"Do Greek women use their behinds to attract?"

"All Greeks attract with their asses," Avigdor said. giggling.

"Some Greeks have other attractions which women appreciate." Nancy offered.

When she said this I withdrew my hand. "We seem to have lost our subject matter because of your white slacks. Come naked next time Nancy and be ignored."

"And display my feminine cruelty promiscuously? What were you three going on about?"

"Various prejudices," I said. "Male chauvinism for one, Jews and the Goyim God, and deeper stuff our friends are stirring in their pot of male discontent."

Both Avigdor and Lucas looked at me.

"The mud stired by racism," I added.

"Under that mud," Avigdor pronounced slowly, "us, a despised people with status, money, a country and courage, still we are a despised people."

"A despised people with everything we don't have," Lucas whispered sadly. "Because we have not secured what you secured we will always be annoyed at the osentatious society of the opulent Jewish bourgeoisie."

"Any bourgeoisie," I cut in, trying to diminish the racial envy emerging..

"You have our God. Now, do you want the money your American Jews have, or believe have?"

"Money as wealth, no, but money for homes and equal education. Money for good food to raise healthy children. Money to keep a good woman. Yes, your God we have, but he is the product not the cause twisting human reason."

Nancy interrupted argument. You boys sound mighty frustrated. For goodness sake accept what life has given you. You were born into what you have. Now, go from there."

"Boys you call us, you lily-white Baptist ridge-runner, projecting a throwback to the southern playland that you were born into."

"Oh Christ, Lucas, don't blame her for that, anymore than you and Avigdor can blame yourselves. We're friends here for gosh sake. What damn words should we use to avoid hurt feelings? White America has always dealt such immeasurable hurt to your people that the use of mitigating labels will not lift one soul from the depths of despair in a city ghetto. Nor will one slaughtered Jew rise from a mass grave."

"It is! Look at your skin color." Lucas insisted, placing his arm alongside Avigdor's arm, "it's darker than mine."

"The desert sun colors me."

"Man, you got the same story a light-colored man uses up north — a darky pretending your kinfolks were farmers burned in the fields and the color carried on to the next generation."

Avigdor's features changed from a puzzled suspicion to a grim smile and nodding of his head

"Big Mac, you amaze me," Lucas said. "If I didn't know you be pagan I could believe you be Christian."

"Negroes of America need more than the philosophy of peaceful resistance that Doctor King preaches.," I told him. You need to eradicate that nervous pressure of race segregation to liquidate the racial inferiority smothering you for three hundred New World years."

Nancy took me up. "They need a Colored Militia in every state as a threat to hold over Whitey. Just the thought that armed Negroes might be called out to insure a colored family moving peacefully into any suburb they can afford will deter ninety percent of the racist whites from coming out to curse at them."

"Hey you sound all right girl. You right on." Lucas beamed a bright smile on her.

"Interesting but naive, Nancy. Lucas knows as well as I do that black politicians, black industrialists, and black establishment people will control such a militia. Should they even propose setting it up to shake the odd white neighborhood it would not add one dollar to a Negro worker's paycheck. It is not political expediency that desegregates but industrial expediency."

She paid no attention to what I said, declaring, "You guys have the tendency of most outcasts to suppose that the lifelines of other people are tamer and more cerebral than your own. Can you not accept that a non-Jew with a white Baptist skin can have the capacity for understanding poverty and racism without suffering it personally?"

Avigdor asked her a strange question for which he did not get a fair answer. Perhaps the question was unfair. "Do you have any conception of what a Jewish soul is or what it ought to be?"

Costa reached between her and Lucas to put a plateau of feta cheese and olives and a carafe of wine on the table. Nancy did not answer Avigdor at once. When she did, her words dropped with a plainsong effect on our watchful silence. "We are cursed with the sins of the dead. It is the life that strangles us. Life where we eject the spiteful juice of creation spit out as love."

I withered hearing that, wondering what she meant. Lucas must have wondered also. He looked puzzled.

When neither Lucas nor I reacted to what Nancy had just said she put her dish aside and motioned for me to pour some wine. "I don't buy this psychic bull," Nancy began. "What I intend and what I mean is that, if there is anything good or bad in a man I mean to find it out."

"To spite or judge us?" Lucas asked.

"We have to judge and accept judgment from one another. If we left this function to the Lord it is no blasphemy to say that our society would very quickly disintegrate."

"Our society of four?" I asked.

"We four are enough. As characters we are a simplification in comparison with the raw reality from which we are hiding."

We four! Like Nancy I felt it too and was warm about us. Maybe it was the ouzo and wine, maybe the atmosphere, maybe her wonderful aura. Whatever it was I wanted it to be meaningful as long as we hung together. "Better leave race and politics off the table tonight or we will never complete the evening together in peace."

"Piece is right," Avigdor agreed. "Back to Nancy long hair. Strip her — her mind that is — in public to advance my study of the American shiska.

"Or retard your study," Don interjected looking at Nancy to see her reaction. "Forward and backwards both good movements," I said. "To escape the lusts of home we have come together here with our betters and worse."

"Balls," Nancy said.

Avigdor struck a priestly pose, hand and fingers blessing the room of diners. "Suffer the horny natives to come unto me for mine are the balls of the kingdom."

"Ethnic freaks the lot of you." Nancy looked right at me saying that. "What I fled was not the lust of flesh. There is flesh anywhere to satiate lust. I fled the victimizing influence of American mini-manhood personified through Billy the Kid to lying Dick Nixon and a host of psychopaths in between. To escape that, born again virgins go to nunneries to play with themselves, and me to Greece to play with you."

She placed her hand on my hand and looked at me, waiting for my reaction.

"They are not the same Nancy. Sex with love does not

always mix well."

Letting go of my hand, Nancy said, "Your gadget is merely an accessory to your love thing, an instrument for pleasure."

Lucas broke in here. "Luckily pleasure is transient."

"Why?"

"If pleasure was permanent grief would be permanent."

Tilting her head Nancy let that statement settle in, then smiled at Lucas, holding out her glass for a refill.

"Do you dream Freudian?" Avigdor asked her.

"Well, Nancyiam, maybe," smiling to herself. "My dreams embrace bodies I cannot accept awake and sober, like unspeakably phallic Turks perpetrating delicious atrocities on my person."

"Lusty stuff," Donald remarked. "When I dream kinky I am still a virgin."

"Virgin? Not in my dreams. In the Ozark hills country kids stop running about twelve years old."

Avigdor was mumbling something. "... suffer the bitches to run onto me for my skirt hides the scepter of rapture."

"You are wounded in the sex Moses man," Lucas said to him.

"Right place for a wound."

"Beautiful freak," Lucas said, turning to me. "I get a great deal more enjoyment contemplating the ethos of this guy's clan than discomfort from the way they behave."

Nancy began to hum, than sing softly, "you only hurt the one you love, the one you shouldn't hurt at all." Then louder through the chorus, her misting eyes moving across Lucas and Avigdor to me. "Sweet little Jesus boy, they didn't even know your name."

Her clear voice had turned off the talking, eating and drinking of the locals. Lucas picked up the words on several verses and they went on together moving to other gospel hymns. He let Nancy finish the last song alone, a Pete Seeger folk verse crying for freedom, democracy and brotherhood.

When she finished, no one applauded. Greek appreciation comes from silent admiration. Taverna guests who liked us being among them sent bottles of ouzo and cognac to our table.

One of the nice things about the Greeks in Plaka was their acceptance of us as though we were nothing out of the ordinary. Not only us, and not only in Plaka. Greeks enjoy all human oddities, even the indispensable idiots in the Levant cities simmering with incest.

Nancy, handsomely female, was a different kind of woman, a talented free spirit whom they would never understand or possess beyond one night.

Greek men could not tolerate that in their women. There is something heavy in a Greek woman's soul, like aching cancer, a substance like ice and fire composed of church and man, superstition and dominance. Not one of us could absorb the sadness and stagnation which dominates their somber world. Greek women will not talk with strangers about their families, their friends and foes. No foreigner is able to invade the repository of the emotions and dreams that color their lives. We can never comprehend the essence of their existence and the eternal struggle they cannot win.

The normal taverna sounds were heard again: spitting, laughing and coughing between puffs on short black cigarettes.

The night scene of local people joined with strangers like us was a vivid mosaic of life.

Then again the setting altered, as if someone had changed a reel. The lights in the district failed and the cafe became pitch dark. Gradually the flames from the cooking spit near the entry helped to reassemble the interior. Candles were brought to the tables. Jokes were flung about in Greek making everyone laugh who understood them. Nancy later told me they were crude remarks about her thin shanks, and Yiannis' gorgeous ell wiggling through olives to slither towards her salad. Until then I had not guessed she was fooling with the mariner, who was not with us that night.

None of us spoke at first. The shadows in the corners playing on our minds cautioned against illicit thoughts. Communication between humans might have its illusions, but there was no doubt about the stark reality of its absence.

Feeling awkward I tried to think of something to say that would be suitable, but the words tumbled empty in my mind. I told myself to hold off and wait for Avigdor to say something strange. Something odd was said, but by Nancy:

"This could be a good time to grope around for a dildo to fill my dream-womb. Your male smell floating in candle smoke is like an opium dream fog."

What made her say that? I felt shame for her like she had risen naked for everyone to see. There was an impulse to go away without her. She seemed to be waiting for one of us to react., looking from one darkened face to another in the candle light.

"Take me to bed in his place," Lucas whispered to Nancy..

"No, I, I can't," shaking her head.

"Not with you, woman. To his room. I feel sick from too much drinking and this candle smell."

Avigdor helped Nancy take Donald outside while I paid our bill. When I caught up, Nancy shrugged, meanng what she we do. I took Lucas' key from his pocket and explained to Nancy how to arrive at Dion's place several lanes away from mine.

Helping Avigdor we got Don up my stairs, undressed him and lifted him into my bunk. Avigdor would stay with him, so I gathered up my toothbrush and an extra blanket and went out to join Nancy.

Lair

Nancy was already asleep in Don's bed when I got there. When I awoke the following morning she was kneeling before a packed bookcase along one wall between the window and a kitchen alcove. Don's robe was draped over her bare shoulders. She turned her head toward me. "What an odd place. Has he read all these books?"

"Most of them, I suppose. He loaned me a few that have his written comments in the margins."

"Does he write?"

"He does scholarly Greek translations."

"No other work?"

"Nothing he gets paid for."

"I thought he might be CIA."

"No, no, he was in consular service. His philosophy is too far left for CIA. They would never hire him, and if they did they would jail him once they know his history."

"Why, what has he done?"

"Umm, kinda wicked stuff by their standards. Nothing

I want to gossip about however. I'll leave that to him."

"He's sharp, like someone who likes to be in charge. Doubt he would tell me much about himself, since he doesn't seem to like me."

"Not true. You as Nancy he likes. But you as white girl U.S.A. he does not like."

"Were I a colored woman with unpleasant American experiences no doubt I would feel the same. Not about white American women, but about you white men. Anyway, I don't like them either."

"Who, Colored men?"

"No, white woman, U.S.A."

"Well, interesting. For me you could be pink Afghanistan and I would still like you."

While talking, Nancy dropped Lucas' robe and came to lie on Don's bed like it was the most natural pose to take, inviting me to explore her.

"You would like me for what? For what I am or what I do with you?"

"The latter. I haven't got you figured yet, Nancy, but how you are is good for me."

"With you?"

"Naturally."

"Then take off Don's pyjamas and get with it."

When I was nude she arched her back for me to slip my leg under her and hook it to the one bent over her waist.

"Leave the lamp on." Locking her hands behind her neck, she looked around the room. "Do you reckon he's had Greek women here?"

"Don't know. Young Greek women are hard to know in

Athens unless they're married or prostitutes. Greek families have peculiar morals. Foreigners can do what they want among themselves but leave Greek daughters alone."

"And sons?"

"Greek sons can do what they like, when they like."

"I know."

"What do you know?"

"Yiannis used to tell me about his school days. In his village he never touched a local girl, but among the guys there was no shame going at one another. After marriage he still went with other men from his village. Their circle dance is fully sex directed. I was permitted after midnight to hang on with the men in a cafe near Sounion. Even I was shocked. The older ones sported like athletes, squatting to tease a man's fly when he wiggled above their face. When the old men wear out the younger ones put them outside with the drunks. Then they tear at each other like dogs, sniffing, groping, pulling out their whoppers. Some even come without jerking off. Normally no woman can witness that. My Greek date put his pistol on the table to warn them not to come after me. I learned later that even a prostitute would leave before midnight. I never went there again."

Telling me this had so aroused Nancy that her head bent low on me, her nails digging into my hips. I eased her away in time so I could delay before lifting her over me.

Rolling on my stomach and chest with her small weight, the points of her breasts rubbing my eyes and lips she kissed me wildly. Then she knelt astride me fitting her vagina over my penis bending it backwards with her writhing. We had a shared climax of super joy.

"You are fun like this," I said, hugging her.

"I love how we are. To be shaken and banged by embrace is the thing I need most."

"Please share your need with me every time."

"When I turn up in Plaka I'll turn on with you, you can be sure."

I did not challenge her reply. I suppose she put it that way for me to understand that her behavior would not be corralled for my pleasure alone.

I went to shower, returning to the bed with one of Donald's shirts that barely covered my groin.

Nancy did not close the bathroom door when she douched. She emerged wearing a colorful Arab robe. "Look what I found on a shelf."

"Beautiful garment. It looks Bedouin."

"Think Don would mind me wearing it?"

"Certainly not, particularly if he could see your bare bum under his robe."

She smiled. "Do you notice what I do about this room?"

"What?"

"This is not a Colored man's place. No family photos, one white girl in a frame posing like a model. There are no Ebony mags, no Earl Jones poetry, no Richard Wright, or Chester Himes books — nothing to show that a Black American lives here."

"Scholars have much the same atmosphere and tastes wherever they live and work I suppose. But there are some deep tomes on the top shelf by learned scholars writing on Black history and philosophy. Doctor Alonzo Turner has one up there. He was a professor of mine at Roosevelt College in

Chicago. Lucas also studied there before I did. Behind the bigger hardbacks are some paperbacks by rebels; Cleaver's "Soul on Ice," Baldwin's "The Fire Next Time" and biographies of Black Power figures."

"Hidden?"

"Out of sight. Greek alien police do not favor radical and political writing whatever the language."

"Why does Don live in Greece alone?"

The expression, 'like us, he's hiding' came to my mouth, but did not slip out. Instead I merely shrugged.

"Married?"

"Lucas?"

"Yes, Lucas."

"Not now. He was."

"Did he leave her back home?"

"His wife died in Chicago when they were involved in that rebellion. Oh, damn it, I said I should not reveal his past, not without his okay."

"You know a lot about him?"

"Too much. For such a short friendship, I know him very well. And his story is unusual, you can believe."

"Tell me?"

"No. Don would not appreciate you knowing what I do unless he chose to tell you himself."

"If I asked him directly would he?"

"He might. In private he could unburden to you like he has with me. Don needs to pour out the fury pent up in his tan soul."

"Behind his color hang-up I see a likeable man. I'll try him, I mean, well, never mind what I mean."

"If your white skin doesn't inhibit him you will learn some startling things. He is likeable as you said."

"Mean too, when he's riled up I bet."

"You're close. Let's just say that his rebellious nature has stirred up some righteous rage among his people in Chicago."

"And you won't tell me?"

"I won't tell you. Ask him."

We did not make love again that morning.

Nancy left to find Yiannis and Avigdor in the market place to select fish they would cook for dinner that evening. I should find them at the cafe in Syntagma Square where we sometimes took morning coffee.

I dressed slowly thinking about the night with her. We had fed each other the beauty-hunger we shared so well. I treasured memories of our love spasms.

Nancy had said something to me one night the week before in my room that still puzzles me. "I make love to use up my time in life, to shatter death before it gets hold of me. I must give everything I can until there is nothing left to give. I dread not having a man when I grow old."

All this from a girl who rarely called fucking other than doing the thing. Looking at the books that challenged Lucas' mind, distorting reality among brutal truth, I thought how throughout human history mankind has derived pitifully little from its existence. One can seldom find or create an enclave of personal peace. We are not saved by politicians any more than by literature.

Wonderfully that morning I was not bothered about the absurd discrepancy between moral values and the facts of human fragility. My contentment that day was based on believing that I had found a warm place for my inner spirit to expand in the company of good friends. It was a rare and brilliant feeling added to my memory.

My partners supposed me to be emancipated and reliable and looked to me with confidence. They were my friends and I was their friend. I felt such adoration for them that giving and receiving became one sentiment.

I found Nancy, Yiannis, Don Lucas and Avigdor outside the café on Syntagma Square where a late winter sun caressed them. At other tables were portly men wearing pajamas and soft slippers, smoking and slurping coffee from miniscule cups.

"We been making an elec for you," Lucas said when I sat down."

"What's an elec?"

"Like an obit, but you since you haven't died yet we composed this to celebrate you alive." Don said.

"The first line is mine," Avigdor interjected: "Shimon you are a goy cousin of the desert, a brother despite your uncut gadget."

"Who's Shimon?"

"My Hebrew name for you."

"Okay. What name you got for me, Don?"

"Soulman. A brother of the ghetto with blue eyes."

Yiannis entered the praise. "You could be Hellenic with your innocent people-love. But guard your soul. Satans tongue strikes from the loins of Zeus and the thighs of women."

"Your people-love is generous but protect your soul." Lucas added. "Watch those with white laws that smother your spirit. Depend on the man to earn what you need, but do not trust him to give you what you want."

"Our Hebrew proverb," added Avigdor, "goes like this. Think always that they depend on thee, but do thou depend only on thyself."

Nancy offered nothing, watching and listening, one hand resting on my thigh. My mind was strong with love and joy for all of us. Jews and Negroes are unbearably sweet when you have known hunger with them, shared danger, quarrelled, made up and made love with them — unbearable when you do not trust them.

In the mist of that Greek morning I hoped for something to strike us magically to permit us to need each other forever. So strongly did this brush me that I felt the earth turn a fraction to reveal another space where love could be seeded.

Down South

There is a ray of fiery brilliance piercing the mass of substance and shadows crowding human souls.

Men like Avigdor Gudinov and Donald Lincoln Lucas are always scorched in life. Donald and Avigdor lived testing the edges of existence. Where Avigdor wrestled demons in his mind and fought Semitic cousins in the desert, Lucas was the demon of his own mind and fought Whitey on the streets of Chicago.

Their emotional energy was invested in their own sects and outbursts of excessive grief could not be expected for a victim who was not a Negro or a Jew. They never felt they were wrong because when honest men think they are wrong they move on.

Don Lucas and I were not together much during the day but many evenings we dined together, talking late into the night in the taverna or in our rooms. I enjoyed those hours with Lucas more than I can casually tell. Talking about himself, his family and people, Lucas' tone was more often affectionate than bitter, sad rather than angry.

When an evening ended it was rare for me not to wonder at the range and emotion of that man's history. He refused to be hived off to that partition called America's Colored, and that is what dictated his mischief. He insisted that we recognize the Black people who are not allowed to thrive as equal humans but as fictional contemporaries in America.

When he left his Southern home for Chicago, Lucas consciously retrieved his faith from Baptist space and decided to put less earthly faith in the Lord. What gave him the guts to do what he did was what I needed to understand.

He told me about his first act of violence in Union Square: "I could not believe the noise after I set off my first blast. I was unable to move. Then there was a deathly aching in my head before I heard the screams. I had done it and things were never going to be the same again."

Before my brown soul-friend revealed more about his role in that bloody Chicago rebellion five years earlier, there were nights of soulful recounting. The most poignant were stories about his Georgia kinfolk.

For Lucas, Mister Charley of the North was a different adversary than Cracker Whitey of the South. He mistrusted our Georgia President's professed love for the Negro. "Carter cloaks his segregationist sins with cowardly pronouncements that down in his basal-bible-balls begets holy ulcers. His gang of disciples in Washington reminds me of that sacred order of brothers who put pebbles in their sandals, suffering their joyful walk across the White House lawn to go down in ecstasy before Whitey's God. Such happy pain you would think to find only in saints of perverted love not in literate racists. That redneck peanut farmer ain't got no more humor than he got lust."

Often in his tales, particularly when referring to Whites whose deportment disturbed him, or to a black when the subject was unpleasant, Donald used his southern dialect. The most moving episodes were stories of his Georgia kinsfolk:

"... An ole Granddaddy done told me about his first boy's wife who got left with six mouths to feed. When her man got sent to a Georgia chain gang for sassin' a white policeman, she took charge. In the four years he be gone, she and my granddaddy took in hungry kids whose folks had died, went to jail or just up and quit.

"What that old man told me got me feelin' shameful. Took me a long time before I could understand how strong that woman was. She be my hero woman when I hear what she done.

"He tell me ...*before two year go by my boy's woman, she be the richest Cullurd Miss in our county. Pretty an' smart too. An' she wern't messin' with low-life Nigras who got no money for what she give, and she don't be stealin' from White Georgia boys who pay good dollar for her black hide twitchin' under em. But oh lawdy the dollars she win with them northern fools, fat Elks, Shriners and the likes of 'em kind comin' to Atlanta for clown paradin'. She slip their purses soon's they drop their pants. Know why she never got rested? Them Yankee pigs be shamed to look the fools they be an' don't go tell the sheriff, you hear what I'm sayin'? And I bet more'n half of 'em pay good for that love-curse she went and got before she took herself to hospital. Them Yankee fools took the curse back North with 'em before knowin' what for they be scratchin'. Her sickness got took back to their wives to cripple white babies in their bellies. It were your Mable's whorin' money what pay your schoolin' up nawth in your Chicago college, you hear me? It were your Aunt Mable got you where you be today in schoolin."*

Those brush strokes on the canvas of Don's life were applied with an innocent and artless voice that disarmed censure.

Taking a sip from his glass Lucas sat back, breathing deeply and making that circular motion with his pink palm rotating toward me.

"For my other granddaddy, my father's pa, shame rested on his land for the eighty-four years he worked it. Two wives, four sisters, five brothers, and three children of his were buried before my Granddaddy passed up there."

Here Lucas raised his eyes beyond my presence. One could feel the shadows of the family who had passed over shading his prayer.

"He was the most sensitive of the old ones who reared me. He was the only elder who could read and write. I was about twelve, maybe, when he said something that never left my mind, something that always checks my feelings when I'm among even the best intentioned Whites.

"There is not in the world's history any record of fruitful dialogue -- no, he said talkin', fruitful talkin' between those who git enough to eat and those who don't. Back then I did not know that there were hungry white children in the states north of Dixie.

"We talked a lot during my growing years. He came close to touching the crux of America's hate-love togetherness, seeing the hybrid population like one big creole family with the young leaving to go north looking for a better life. He got across to me that in the complex modern America, individuals were more enmeshed with one another than they believed.

"He warned that I had a devil temper. You ain't like most of us, he told me. You won't stay a boy till you reach forty then be called Uncle by rednecks who choke up trying to call a Colored man by his family name.

"I'm climbin' a high mountain to git home," he would say."

... gettin' ovah all right in this life, but heaven is callin'. My old eyes be closin' but your young black eyes been watchin' what this nation doin' to us. You young'uns be fit to burst. But you all don't be ready yet, you hear what I'm sayin?. Keep it inside for a spell. And don't be thinkin' out loud down here. When a cullurd home boy be talkin' like a man in this county he kin wind up dead. Get intelligent first. The best an' smartest be survivin'.

What been forced on cullurds for so long killed off the weak ones. You strong ones be the best — hunnerds of you in every south'n county and nawth'n ghetto, strong, mean Nigras who be smart. Find 'em, work and plan. Force white man to stand off. Don't be stupid by showin' guns. you hear what I'm sayin'? Git a heap a learnin' and vote. Doin' it right jest might get the God-equal life we be titled to. And don't be doubt'n America ain't the best place for it. It can happin' here. An' you Danny Lincoln kin help it happin', I know.

Don's face seemed younger in the dim taverna. He grinned like the young boy who a generation earlier listened to his old grandfather.

"Well, Mac my friend, you can understand how worked

up I was, how anxious to become educated, how impatient to find others like me who would do something to lift our people from their misery. One summer back home, Granddaddy asked what I was learning in Yankee land. He saw how uncomfortable I was just working a bit around the farm and not going to town. I told him it was less learning than unlearning. Our lot was not going to improve much through Whitey's goodwill. It took me all my first year at Roosevelt College to see through the fourflushers who say they are liberal but won't rent a room to a Negro student. Something wasn't right about a nation's claim on moral worth and Christian belief that has no place for common humanity.

Humanity ain't common, Donny. He said to me...*them Nawthn' liberal folk spread it around like mule droppins' cause they calculatin' to use you. The Nawth profits off y'all. Profitin' is what they pray for. That be the white man's gawd.*

"Good thing you haven't been North, I said to him. You would cry blood if you saw those city ghettos filled with maimed, neglected, ill-educated and angry kids. It's not their own who neglect them, but the powers in control who poison their human well being. It's an incredible nasty political design. City blacks are stuttering with rage."

You gettin' a hard education Donny. First time I heard you say Blacks instead of Cullurd or Negra. Black is beautiful, ain't that what y'all say up there?

"Not so beautiful up there Grandpa. For a hungry, uneducated man, colored or white it is hell-grinding dirt. Profitism, you said. That boss creed needs poor people scared for their jobs who can't afford not to work for a dollar an hour."

You so right Donny. But Nawth'n prejudice be deeper

than money. Whitey up there be fearin' Cullurd folks. Improvin" your mind means you be dis-improvin' theirs. It's why they be so mean. Be patient and study boy. Don't trust white folks up Nawth, an' not many Negras either. Believe everybody depends on you, but you be dependin' only on yourself.

Lucas put down his drink. When telling me stories about his past he rarely drank much. Even a mild debauchery would affront their memory.

"My granddad's warning shook me up. I already opened up to a couple of guys I thought I could trust. It hurt a lot of us Urban Cubans when we whipped Mayor Dinky's ass, and almost won over the whole damn city against the police and state militia."

Well, this surprised me. I would never have suspected my friend's heavy involvement with the rebellion. Here was this soft-spoken, handsome Donald Lincoln Lucas calmly telling me that he fought in the bloodiest racial conflict since World War Two in our native Chicago.

"What was your part? You were not the rebellion leader called Lincoln, were you?"

Lucas merely smiled, raising his eyebrows as if surprised that he had told me as much as he did. "I guess I need the odd white guy like you for a friend to balance my own racial bias. But never mind me. I loved my old Grandmother who was a former slave's child. We were not always sure she understood what we spoke about. She was looking in bible most of the day, once in a while looking up, wondering aloud if being up north was doing me any good. She did not like those free Negroes and the liberal Whites I hung out with up there. "She said to me,

I can't like Nawthn' Yankees a thousand miles up from Georgia stirrin' you up to face a lynch mob.

"I like thinking that I'm working myself up to have the mob facing me, Grandma. Haven't yet worked how it will come about but before I'm through up there, before I'm through...

"But she was no longer listening, turning pages of her old bible and praying, blocking out temporal prophecies for the wisdom of older prophets in her faith.

"That fine brown woman knew it was her time to leave this world. My granddaddy was soon to follow. Just before he died he took me to visit all the graves of our kinfolk. We walked away from each plot without a backward look after kissing the headstone, or the ground when there was no marker. He died quietly, my mother holding his hand while my daddy read from Grandma's bible through the night. When they passed over it seemed like everyone but my mother got in a hurry to follow."

Lucas raised his head, his thoughts way beyond Plaka: "My other granddaddy, then his wife, my mother's twin sister, and an uncle passed over. Two cousins of mine were killed in Korea. My brother Jimmy came back all shot up and went into preaching. Never got much out of him about how it was there.

"My daddy, like both my grandfathers was southern black. He was old when I finished college. I was his youngest son. No, let me be honest — I'll tell you something only my daughter knows and certainly my mother. I was not the true son of Mamma's husband. Momma and him were not together when she took up with a white man. She got me born from that man on purpose. My sister told me that Mamma had no regrets because by her thinking, if I would be kinda white then life might be easier for me. I know who my real father is, but I wont say who he is right now.

"My mother never told me. But when her husband came back home, he did.. He was afraid that I would hate my mother if I learned the truth outside the family. He was not strong on genetics but he was unmatched for kindness.

"My reaction, that I didn't let on about, was one of delight mixed with doubt. I was different from my brothers and sisters and a heck of a lot lighter, like high-yellas who become doctors iin he big cities. I grew up feeling superior because of that. And I did go further, with big ideas and ambition to get decently educated. I guess my mother's idea was sound. I spawned a mighty white daughter with Elaine, a virgin kid I met in college. Elaine passed over borning her. That tore my soul terribly."

He raised his head to look full at me, his dark eyes blinking back tears. "The noble and godly folk of my youth all passed over except my daughter passing for white." His eyes shifted to the ceiling. I imagined his thoughts rising to the heavens above the Acropolis. "All passed over."

He held his drink, and was silent for some time. "Though I am city wise now I identify more with the migrant Negroes who work share-cropper farms. My youth was forged in the depths of their hard life. Our spirituals, our folk tunes and blues cry of the things that hurt, and the God that soothes us. When you get home again go to a Southside church. Listen to the preacher's call and the congregation responding. It's talkin' and testifyin' between the preacher and his church flock. . This talk and response goes on in the ghettos too with street talk instead of bible stuff. Our African tradition does not divide the sacred and the secular. There is no formal line between performers and audience. During slavery the field workers were the audience. The field was the church. The leader has the calling to sing out. The workers respond the same as in the tabernacles up north. A good leader keeps the audience — a good preacher too. Poor ones lose us. They have to involve us or we don't hear them rightly."

Sighing deeply Lucas let me fill his glass again. We drank together in silence. I could see that it was also the women of his life who got him through to that space in Athens where I met him. Emotions that had come and gone like images on life's screen were stilled. Reflected in his tan face was the conscience of America that was just beginning, a century after the Civil War, to loosen the knots of prejudice.

Donald Lincoln Lucas deserved more than a crumbling world, a dead wife, and a daughter passing for white spawning white babies.

Vania and Sam-Sam

The first Saturday of spring was mild, a pale yellow sun touching the cold stone pillars of the Parthenon. Lucas was restless, he could not stay indoors working on anything, and was away from Plaka most afternoons strolling the streets of Athens. He was telling me about a couple of New York fatsos who were curious about him, asking why he was in Greece.

"I had no objection to their asking about things concerning me. One has to have a certain curiosity about a Colored man who was a writer, that's what I said I was. I linked Greek tragedies to American happenings, human things about grief, calumnious events and venal gossip about power folk in America who make the lives of America's Coloreds so hard. It is only natural I told them, when they asked me why I confide so emotionally, that if their attention is drawn to a lone Black man in a foreign place then they should know why I fled their land of non-plenty, and no-mercy and emphasize with my plight.

"Is it wise to rake up that past, the little fat woman asked me. I looked straight into her eyes and said that it was better than raking up dry bones from darkies you've lynched. Penguin eyes burst when I tell them that. Then I bow my head and tell 'em, when you be buried in your all-whitey cemetery I will come pay respects and tenderly spray nigger-pee over your plastic flowers. By the time they have that worked out my dark dicky is splashing blessings over their cow sandals. Man how they curse and dance about. Then they spill out those sweet racist poems stored thick in their pink heads that they hadn't the nerve to recite before I got them het up."

The recipients of his sprayed blessings showed up at Taverna Diogenes that weekend. I was entering at the same time when a really heavy man, and a short roly-poly woman jammed in the doorway blocking my way. The woman was saying to the big guy, "There he is Sam-Sam -- pissin' sambo with a white chick, and another weirdo at that table."

"I want to talk to him," Sam-Sam the husband replied. "Grab that empty table behind them while I order us steaks."

She waddled past Greeks who could hardly believe the sight: lynch pin legs in suede boots widening into enormous buttocks and hips, a saggy stomach, pendulous breasts, and thick neck supporting her powdered round face and golden wig.

Her husband was trying to order food from the cook. "Hey chef, you know English? American-English? Two of those big steaks. No make it three on one plate, well done and a dozen roast potatoes. Damn it, cook, I'm ordering."

"You should give the waiter your order," I told him. "Less confusing for the chef. He'll have thirty steaks to do within this half hour before dinner, and he takes pride grilling them right."

"Oh, okay, thanks. Which one is the waiter? That him?"

"Yeah, Costa. Point to where you'll be sitting and he will get to you." With that, I walked towards the back tables with fatso following me.

His wife had already plunked her toady torso on a chair behind Nancy, buttocks hung over the edges, her neck and bust all of one piece rolling down to a ponderous stomach.

Fat Sam was massive, shoulders abnormally wide, a florid formless face glistening with ill-health. Thick wrists and sausage fingers with dark hairs sprouted from the back of his hands. From his collar a curly mat grew up to his greying hair. Yellow-brown goat eyes peered from sinks of fat. He was a grunter and a watcher, letting his wife do the trivial talking. He stared at Lucas who paid no attention to him.

Fatsy wife had already cocked her head towards Avigdor, Nancy, and Don trying to catch their conversation.

"Have you two slept together yet?" Avigdor asked Nancy, returning to their topic after greeting me.

"No."

"Why not?"

Nancy shrugged, pursing her lips.

"Would you do it?"

"Do what? A Colored guy or a Jew?"

The wife leaned towards Nancy, pointing to Donald. "Him."

Nancy had been alerted by Lucas that these two were the ones he peed on. Grinning, Nancy replied to the woman. "Maybe, if the urge and opportunity collide."

"Would he object?" Avigdor pointed to me.

"We share our bodies and spirits, not own each other," I told him.

Avigdor turned to Nancy. "Now you have permission."

"Thanks, but one in a gang is my usual rule. I'm no groupie."

"What is a groupie?" Avigdor queried, shaking his head.

The fat wife broke in here: "A chick who sleeps with the whole band," she told Avigdor, then thrusting her pudgy finger towards Nancy, addressed her, "What are they trying to do honey, gang group you?"

"Don't do incest. These are my psychic-soul brothers. Do you want one of them?"

"No offense honey. Just want to get acquainted. I'm Vania and Sam-Sam here is a lawyer. We're Americans. You too I think. Where you from? Detroit, Chicago?"

"New York," I said.

"All three of you?"

"I mean you. Your talk gives it away."

"Right, we're New York geezers from the Bronx, out of Brooklyn. Best place for culture in America, concerts and everything. Good place for making money too." Turning to Avigdor, "She said something about a Jew? You Jewish?" Looking at Avigdor. "Talk Yiddish to him, Sam-Sam."

"Your name is peculiar," Avigdor said to her.

"Rosen? What is funny about Rosen? Ordinary name really. How did you know our name?"

"Vania, it means distress in Hebrew."

"Oh, you're Hebrew, I mean Israeli. Tel Aviv? Jerusalem? We go there next month to the Zionist International Women's Congress. You a Zionist?"

"No way, " Nancy said, "not him."

"Oh. Political then, Mapai, the Labor Party? Not right

wing I'm sure. Wouldn't be mixing with liberal persons like this American kid and a Colored boy — er, person. You're not religious either, there are no spit curls around your ears. With those light eyes your family must be from Russia."

"British occupation," Avigdor said. "My grandma was a slut for British officers."

"What a thing to say about your babushka. What occupation? Not strong on politics. Democrats and Republicans are enough for one country. Keeps America great when politics are simple, don't you agree?"

No one answered. Perhaps none of us agreed.

Actors, I thought, this blimp with her elephant mate playing the Yiddisher Mama, savoring our pornographic scene. She was not coming over the way she thought. Her kind probes superficially, pretends to listen then hits below the belt. I was on my guard.

One could not caricature the Rosens for they were caricaturing themselves. What astonished me was that they were intelligent, quick in their perceptions, and yet seemed to be quite unconscious of their own absurdities. Fucking useless whites, shameless and grotesque was my initial view of them. They seemed like dregs from the lawyers' guild and private clubs, boozing with other smug members who suffer from emotional indigestion at the thought of their children away at university sleeping with blacks and goyim.

I was wrong.

The evening turned out more interesting than I expected. We had a good go at the Rosens, partly in fun, partly serious, debating about liberty and tyranny with an even spread of second-rate vanity. Liberty from what and for what? And tyranny from what and for what? They held up very well. Though I did not like them more when we separated, neither did I like them less.

"Eat," Sam ordered his wife.

Vania turned away with a grin, nodding that she would carry on after they put away their kilo of meat and potatoes.

We four then played wild with odd topics as though they were not there. Not quite right — we hoped to wound their sensitivity if not their appetite. We succeeded with neither.

"You mean you took that little male like a Turk?" I began, looking at Lucas.

"Tasteful little Auklet," Lucas said.

"You're a freak," Avigdor told him.

"We all are. The Aegean is a brothel bazaar for visiting freaks." Don purposely looked at Sam-Sam and Vania.

"You males," Nancy said, "whore with your minds every waking hour."

"At least half the time," I told her. "More men sleep with their peers than women sleep with theirs?"

"Sleep?"

"Pointless whether male inter-love is natural or not. Like religion, it's accessible," Donald offered.

I did not understand what Nancy said next.

"A human's impulse is to arrive at something higher than a natural state."

"Salome dar-r-ling, you're positively lewd," Avigdor said, giggling.

"Hey, label me Aphrodite. I want to feel Greek."

"You want to feel Greeks?" Avigdor reached behind to take a bottle of cognac from a basket, pulling the cork out with his teeth.

"A Christian privilege this cognac, luxury like asparagus out of season." He took a long draught from it before signalling Costa for fresh glasses, holding up six fingers.

Six glasses? I was annoyed that he would treat the Rosens to our cognac, even though it was a free bottle sent to our table by other diners in the taverna.

"What small luxuries do you favor, Donny?"

It was the first time I heard Nancy address Lucas that way. Lucas answered her. "The unhearing Gods of myth accompanying me, a climate of sun, books, ancient scrolls, Greek bathouses, and five nubile munchkins caressing my sepia jewels."

"Great achievements stem from small luxuries," I said to him, "I think sometimes that you are almost there, Donald. Overcome a few more obstacles and you will make it."

He shook his head, sighed and sipped from the drink Avigdor had poured for him. "One can seldom find or rarely create an enclave of placid privacy." He looked towards the fat pair whose heavy necks were curved over their plates.

"If an inner man wants to be left alone he should be left alone," Nancy said.

Nancy had made me aware that Lucas had already encountered the Rosens. From what I heard when they came in, they did not know that Lucas was in Taverna Diogenes. Nancy seemed to sense that his anonymity was threatened because of them.

I told Avigdor to stop gulping from that bottle, and fill our glasses. " The way you guzzle that stuff you will sure-n-hell end your days in Gomorrah along with me with me and

Don."

"Paradise," Avigdor chanted, raising his arms to the ceiling: "*Shami ma im bak shu, rakha mim alai.*"

"What the hell is that?" Vania Rosen asked, her mouth sucking the last morsel of meat fat.

"Bialik," I told them. "A fine Hebrew poet. Your wife's favorite, isn't he, Avigdor?"

"He wrote like a Greek," Lucas said.

Avigdor's eyes misted as he sipped from the bottle again. "There appeared a chariot and horses of fire on the whirlwind, and he went up to heaven on the power of my gaze."

"Oh Christ," I said.

"Yes?"

"Stop playing the Nazarene masochist. You would not look well in a skirt among his twelve man-maidens."

Avigdor brought the bottle down hard on the table, shaking the glasses. "Nothing humorous in that blasphemy."

"Anathema," Vania blurted out.

"Enema," Avigdor shouted.

"Anathema, shit," Nancy pronounced.

"Dear people, strange people," Vania said softly, "you are all so prone to fantasy. The roots may be found in your ancestry as well as in the tilted cultural mores of our America."

"Crap, Mother Bronx," Lucas said. "You're trapped in the mire we opted to get unstuck from — the gag end of Judeo-protestant ethics that twists the teats of human indifference to milk us dry. You applaud the clown jesters of government, ejaculating patriotic images with fireworks on kiss America days, like the middle-class wasps."

"Virtuous sentiments. Why should we not ride with

them? You know something better?"

"Why better? Just different."

"Like what?"

"Like whatever we need beside sustenance and shelter, like a loving companion, and space for creativity."

Here Fat Sam pursed his lips, making vague gestures with his left hand, muttering through clenched teeth. "Has this guy got you on dope, or what?" He looked to Nancy for her reaction.

Nancy was smiling without further comment.

This made me start. For the first time I saw Big Sam as some sort of police agent.

"What do these misfits do for you?" Vania asked Nancy, looking from Lucas to me. Her 'misfits' sounded as if she meant pimps.

"These are good guys, funny, serious men — crazy now and then, and why shouldn't they be? The world in which we survive has become artful in its wickedness, and the banality of cooperate greed has become ever more subtly disguised as virtue. These guys, like me, are copping out."

"Bizarre cop-out," lawyer Sam-Sam murmured, finally entering the fray. "Vice can disguise itself as virtue. What do you want in your inner world?"

Nancy thought for a moment, her eyes closed, grimacing. "To understand the mystic element probing our guts."

Big Sam, breathing heavily, rolled his eyes and shook his head.

"But what do you get from them Nancy?" Vania insisted.

Nancy was still smiling. I was sure she would breath out some erotic whispers about aberrant sexual conduct, or some such oddment. Instead she attempted to hide her feelings about us and not confide what was deep inside her generous body.

"They leave me be my own person. Morally and sexually I am wholly myself, free to behave how I feel with whomever I choose. It is rare to be in the company of men who do not judge me."

"This is what you want?"

"Far better than what I've known, Vania."

"A dangerous remedy for a girl your age to seek an escape through chaotic imagery of the dreaming mind, hoping it will comfort your daily existence. I can't imagine permitting the unconscious darkness to rise above the mind's horizon to merge with this world we live in."

"What danger do you see in that?" I asked Vania.

"You can't make the world better in this foreign place," her husband interrupted.

"Why better, just different." I replied directly to him. "Your American world has become more criminally crafty in its wickedness, and the banality evil..."

"Your girll friend already said that." Sam cut in. "Vice can disguise itself as virtue," he repeated. "Have they taught you anything different?"

"You alread said that," I said, mocking his tone. "What they have taught me is how difficult it is to see true virtue in a world devoted to so many elaborations of deception."

"Like how?"

"To trust my own philosophy, to rise above racist

nationalism."

"This is what you want?"

"No worse than what I've known."

"Bizarre thinking. What else do you want?"

"Like Nancy I want to explore the mystic element of human nature."

Big Sam raised his eyebrows, and patted his stomach as if in thought.

"What do you see as dangerous in that?"

"No remedy," Big Sam insisted, "like drug inspired visions, no applicative meaning, no conceivable purpose — nothing whatever to do with what you do nor how you think or feel."

"Exactly. Having nothing to do with how we act, think, or feel."

"Mythic hucksters — spirit mongers. Hazardous and vicious because it leads untutored victims like Nancy here to believe that something profound is being said when scarcely anything of value is offered." Stopping there, Big Sam sat back in his chair that began to crack under his weight.

Donald, addressing Sam for the first time, said softly, "You are looking for a theological meaning to our life style. It is not only by theology that spiritual hunger is fed."

Puffing his thick lips, Big Sam snorted.

Vania did not seem to know how to go on, or chose not to debate ideas beyond her secular space. She seemed less mystified with Nancy's views while the men attempted to match wits. I sensed that she even liked Nancy. By now, Sam had taken another chair. He and Vania moved their chairs toward us. They were too big to actually squeeze in at our table. Vania clung to Nancy like a censoring mother.

"You are religious, aren't you? Some branch of religion with belief in God?"

"Converted Catholic through family planning, that kind of Catholic," Nancy lied.

"Baptized Catholic?"

"Saved and sanctified with rosy baby-pee."

"Rosy what?"

"Pee-pee, like in the basins in Rome and cathedrals west when they splash cold water on the kid. That'l make anyone pee."

To her credit Vania did not fall for that nonsense.

"Are you in one of those weird cults?"

"No, no. Nothing that kinky. For my tribe Jesus was a dark Jewess. Mary remains the abused adultress luring her miraculous son's father to seduce her."

For ten seconds Vania was silenced. Nancy's words she had heard. But their meaning? Closing her eyes she tried to understand, but lost it. Opening them she appealed to Sam-Sam to sort Nancy out.

"Having us on, as the British would say," Sam remarked, rising to stretch and look towards the back of the room.

"Oh Sam-Sam, are we leaving?"

"Bathroom," he whispered. Costa intercepted him before he fell into the wine cellar, pointing to a back door and crooking his forefinger to signal that Sam must go outside the building to find the toilet shack.

Her husband out of sight, Vania leaned towards Lucas. "Did you fill this youngster and her old boyfriend with the discrepancy between the idea of absolute values and the facts of human frailty?"

From what tome did she get that topic heading, I wondered?

Don raised his eyes to me. "Tall man is filling her with ethereal spermatozoa, not me."

"Blue Eyes is no spiritualist," she said, looking at me. "There's no cloud of silver dust around him." Turning back she looked Donald up and down, searching something hidden in his handsome face or elsewhere.

"Who are your friends in Greece other than these hippy types? Who are they? Where are they? I can't see how these three offer much stimulus for a scholar like you. And I do not believe what I heard about a Turkish boy and you, nor that you have not fulfilled this dream girl's dream. I bet she was curious to check rumors about you colored men, like I am."

"I be aware of that. Your toes been checkin' out my crotch ever since you turned this way." Don responded.

"Sam-Sam has a hard time making with the ready. Get it, never really hard."

"Never hard Sam the kosher man," I quipped. "Maybe Don ain't cut."

Vania ignored me.

"I'll treat a big night in Pireaus — luxury hotel and all the works. You game?" She smiled with well cared for teeth, then frowned when Lucas shook his head.

"No disrespect but count me out. My senses are well treated. I am saved, sanctified and satisfied. I surround myself with my close friends and share my emotional needs with them."

"Sex?" she prompted, grinning at Nancy as if she shared the same big cock myth about Negro genetalia.

Moving his hand in a circle to dismiss the point she

wanted to make, Lucas said, "I love my beloved friends. I take and use them like they take and use me. Anyone else I send home after breakfast the next morning."

"I like you. You are not devious by instinct, not hard to take close up."

I wondered how Donald would respond to that? Before he did, Vania turned to Nancy.

"I am curious about you — sex isn't that important is it Nancy?"

"Isn't it? From the way you are groping for it I wonder. If it is not important Mrs. Bronx, your behavior is most odd. My conditioning claims that a great deal of it is vital to happiness and sanity." Nancy stretched her arm towards me, raising her hand to my lips. Vania glanced at me and back to Nancy then lowered her head, her chin folding into her neck, robbed of sexuality by Nancy's blunt rebuke.

"Disease and heartbreak," she muttered.

"Slippery and suspicious, my New York cousins via Polanski," Avigdor said.

She raised her head sharply, directing a sharp look at him.

"Drink this, you're in heat," he said, holding out a glass of cognac.

She took it, drained the glass, and at once shook off her posture of disappointment and toasted us: "Zionist renegade and two soul thieves consensually raping this American Flower Child," reaching out to touch Nancy's hand. "You're not Catholic, and certainly not Jewish. Baptist spirituality radiates from you."

Laughing, Nancy nodded that she was right. "I'm all

saintly for these disciples. Mary the Mother, Mary Magdalene the Christ wife, Lilith the early strumpet — all the pioneer power dames, the whole fabric to comfort earth's men."

Avigdor: "Mogen David covering our privates..."

Lucas: "Chanting the Hallelujah Chorus..."

My remark: "Jesus Christ, super spies."

"Make a weirdo record," Nancy said, cutting into our chorus.

"Chant in Hebrew now you minstrels. "Vania's voice almost choked. She took Avigdor's drink and swallowed whatever was. in his glass. "Peace and joy is what I seek, and so should you," Vania pleaded. "Why are you doing this? Your anti-establishment and Semitic nonsense drooling from your rolling tongues, your mouths snarling like Polish dogs baying after a Treblinka Jewess is frightening. Why do you want to hurt? What are you trying to prove?"

"That nothing is sacred big Mama, neither your sex hunger nor our suffering, or the other way around. Don't probe my womb and we won't probe yours."

Nancy's offer might have reformed the gap between Vania and us had Avigdor let her be.

She had not addressed Avigdor once since her husband went out to the john.

Now Avigdor cruelly addressed her. "Vania, you are wounded in the crotch. A kike wound, you got a kike wound." He seemed pleased with that cruel image.

"Well that's all right, if that is what you want to think. Even funny, very funny." Vania was not smiling, but neither was she angry. It was as though she heard the slurs and discounted them, like she discounted the Hebrew traitor mocking her. Back in the Bronx they were the renegades in her social routine that she registered automatically, like the prisoners slaving in concentration camps registered the arrivals and departures of prisoners without really seeing them.

"I'm sorry for you. A Sabra living in an unreal cloud, unable or unwilling to explore beyond it. You're an innocent Jew who really doesn't know how merciless is hate-power, how cruel, how unbelievably cruel Europe was to our people."

And there, taking another drink, Vania ended it, turning off the flow as nimbly as one turns a valve. "What is keeping Sam-Sam? Hope he didn't fall in."

Donald abruptly got up and headed towards the side door, disappearing towards the outdoor latrine.

We drank in silence, each tasting our thoughts with the cognac. I swished it around in my mouth and felt it smart my gums. The aroma rose in my head with sweet fumes.

Vania lowered her glass and looked into the eyes of Avigdor, stretching her arm on the table towards him, her white hand closing over his desert brown hand, pink fingers caressing his knuckles. It was a motherly gesture so old and tender that Avigdor felt it like a stroke on the foundations of his life. Sighing, Avigdor did not draw his hand away from her touch.

Returning from the outhouse, Big Sam filled the back door, his fly still open. With an inquiring bearing he came straight towards Nancy. His glare was a typical lawyer's expression of censure towards a free mind, and because Nancy was thin and young, a fat man's leer of lust.

I grit my teeth knowing that if a big man like that ever forced himself on her she would suffer.

Lucas' absence took over. "Your friend not returning?"

he asked me.

I shrugged.

"He's gone out'a sight. Sprinklin' blue suede shoes maybe," Vania said to him.

Avigdor did not get the joke.

Sam-Sam sat down in the chair Lucas had occupied. "Are you all right, Vania?"

She nodded.

"Your face is flushed. They been bugging you?"

"Bugging her?" Sam ignored me.

Vania sighed heavily, holding up her glass to suggest that drink might be the cause of her complexion. Her breasts strained the blouse that barely contained the fat. "We played charades, offering love under labels of hate. Each actor believing their own truth, each character a...."

"For Christ sake Vania stop masturbating in public. That extremity of human misery your family suffered is beyond the conception of people like these. The camps are closed. Stop opening the holocaust gates for strangers to snoop around. It's obscene."

Fucking bully, I thought, seeing Vania wilt under his pressure. Vania had extraordinary powers of simplicity and that basic will to survive which was exhibited over and over again by survivors of the Nazi camps who populate Israel today. Her husband would not permit her catharsis, the art we served Lucas day after day. No doubt Sam had nagged her to efface the concentration camp number they burned into her skin and soul, the scar on her wrist a sick reminder of both cruelties.

He was as incapable of conceiving the hardship Vania and Lucas went through every day of their childhood, as he was incapable of imagining pain or danger to himself.

"What is he called, your Colored friend?" Sam asked Nancy.

"Ask him yourself."

Then he asked me what Lucas does.

"The same as we do, nothing. We did not come here to do anything."

"And Nancy, have you come here for nothing?"

"Nothing is nothing," Nancy replied with some impatience. "I found new friends here. That was something. Why do you ask?"

"Wasting your youth," Vania said before her husband could reply to Nancy. "You should be back home studying, and setting up your future."

"Future for what? To become a Miss Profit Mother producing children for male chauvinists to order into your materialistic wars for the glory of manifest destiny?"

"America is strong because of decisions like that," Big Sam broke in. "Democracy is safe for dissenters of your sort. No doubt you will teach your children to mock it. The United States was respected in this world without question until you traitors began knocking it abroad."

"Traitor? Will you give me a hundred dollars for each of my war medals?"

Sam looked startled rather than skeptical, turning to Nancy who held up five fingers to count five medals confirmg that I was a combat soldier in the war that halted the European slaughter.

"Since World War Two our global behavior is one of cunning coarseness built on the rationale of manifest destiny proscribed in your CIA Bible. It ropes us so firmly on the cross of righteousness that it is no longer indecent to arm dictators who rain American made bombs on nuns, babies, and crippled old men."

"Well, well, another dangling dissident running down the homeland. Thank Christ you left to make room for good immigrants who want to live there. In Russia they would lock you up in a nut house."

"America is the biggest Gulag there is for the disadvantaged. Mis-education, under-nourishment and segregation creates dismal people. People and health are at least equal in importance as profit and two cars. The world sees super-America differently than you want to believe; brutal when it blunders, inhuman when it profits, bedding down with generals with a violent ideology when it is good for American business."

"Good speech," Sam applauded. "The eloquence of failure. Free white and forty-something with your gullible girlfriend. You haven't made it with your unholy wasp class so you escape to this level hoping to exculpate yourself from the stigma of of ailure. You don't deserve to go back home."

"In a gone rotten free world with secular ambition — with ruthless greed and dishonesty raised to a principle of action, your plea for the holy and sacred *'love it or leave'*, your gory western democracy is out of order, Mister Lawyer."

"You cannot sustain a theory of society without a theory of knowledge. What are you anyway, a third world agent?"

"I know less what about I am than what I am not. I am not a bigot, nor a political aesthete."

"We are not aesthetes."

Lucas could not be a silent listener any longer. "The hell you're not," accusing Rosen directly. "It's transparent; the empty aesthetic elitism of officialese, linked to the hollow glitter of secret service fascism. CIA is lit like neon across your overstuffed corpse."

"Strange bootleg suspicion. Is that why you think I am here?"

"Your aura is heavy man, heavier than you look, weighted by sinister curiosity, not by any central fascination for a displaced colored man."

"My parents were immigrants. My wife was a refugee. You should be proud to be American. If there is something to change in America it will not be done from a Greek wine house."

"Change? White America wants no change fur us Blacks. The basic evil of inequality is a change you dread. I despise how America beats down its minorities: Hispanics, Natives, and my people. The depressed minorities back home need change. For them no alteration could be for the worse. You don't know how to relate to non-Jews as equals. You're either on the throne of Zion looking down on the drone worker-goyim, or so disordered from centuries of ostracism that you walk with head down telling the world to let you be, enough of you have been killed. But who counts the Southern dead black people, dating from slavery through the klan era to the organized political lawlessness of Jim Crow and poll tax racist games that the white charlies still play into this century. The quality of our suffering has been no less dramatic than yours."

"Don't blanket me with that," Vania said. "I am active on behalf of New York minorities. Our Zionist-Liberal Ladies maintain philanthropic enterprises in their neighborhoods. I like Colored people, their spirituals, their smiles. I am a minority myself, and I feel for them — I really do."

"How are you feeling him?" Avigdor asked, slurring his words. "Your hands are on the table." He leaned down to peer under, nearly falling from his chair.

I interrupted here because Don was getting too worked up. I motioned for him to go with Costa to the wine celler and choose the tavernas best wine. Then, turning to the Rosens, "What you two are expressing is the feel-good view of your comfortable in-group, avoiding the truth of Donny's bleak and deprived life."

"Well, for God's sake. Did you hear that Sam-Sam? What does he know? What does he know?" Flapping her short arms around, flesh flapping, her mind distraught, Vania was unable to form a coherent reply.

Lucas emerged from the celler with two bottles. He placed one bottle before Sam Rosen, and the other by me. Then, placing his hands on Vania's shoulders, he whispered sometning to her and sat down beside her.

Smiling, she turned to look at him.

Lucas returned her smile warmly, saying softly as though to a child, "Your antecedents wore the same grinning masks as mine to conceal the fear and rage tearing at their guts. Your Zionist leaders, like our Black politicians sold their honor to buy escape for their colleagues. But your rabbis and our preachers hung in with their people. Your faith did not save six million of you, but it won you a homeland. Our faith back home in the ghettos and on the tenant farms have not produced the material with the spiritual like it has for you.

"We have tried many ways to beak the bonds of segregation using boycotts, riots, rebellions, black power resistance, and the Muslim faith that many young Coloreds are embracing. And still we are a long way off."

Sam Rosen interrupted Lucas, pronouncing rather smugly. "we have never abandoned our peaceful God and that is why we have prevailed."

"Easy there, Sam-the man. Your biblical history is soaked with the blood of your adversaries. It wasn't Moses who blasted the King David Hotel in your holy city blowing the British Command to hell. And I must warn you that the new young bloods, who are our children, attracted to the new forces crowding our traditional religions, may not have the patience we had when we marched peacefully with Reverend King in Alabama."

"We know that some people hate us, but I refuse your hatred. Hate will only turn inward."

"I'll concede you that, Sam but every conflict that has not been suffered to the end and resolved will reoccur. And your children will not deserve their fate."

"What fate?" Sam Rosen asked.

"When we stop smiling our children might kill your children." Turning his face upward, sighing, Lucas looked up to some heaven beyond us, and for that moment we were not there with him. "Man alone must face his loneliness and yet must love his errant neighbor." Then slowly shaking his head, an expression midway between despair and resignation transformed his dark face into a grim smile.

Sam leaned toward Donald and puckered his lips. "If you don't kill us you will kiss us. Tell me, when have you ever heard of a gang of colored kids burning a synagogue? It has never happened, and I doubt that it ever will happen."

Lucas couldn't help smiling while nodding his head in agreement.

"Such a kind man when you're not angry," Vania said to Lucas, unable or unwilling to deal with his meaning. Nothing would get into her insular head.

Nancy told Vania, "You would not recognize a truly happy Negro because you never made one happy. They have a splendid intimacy with the holy spirit that no other faith can match."

Big Sam's fleshy jewels shook when he labeled Nancy the all America cliché shiska.

"What do you get from them?" Vania asked her.

"Great bursts of selfish joy."

"Whoops!" Avigdor screeched, slopping drink into his glass spilling some on Rosen's fly. Sam reached out, his strong fingers gripping Avigdor's arm while he plucked the bottle from his shaking hand.

Vania looked at her husband. "How does she mean that?"

"Don't be unduly concerned, matzo-mama," I said mockingly. "We are impeccably moral. We smoke for dreams and fuck for peace. All other dolor rejected."

"Dollar?"

"She means pain, Vania. The pain our affluent type are believed not to be acquainted with. We manage however, better than her companions."

Don spoke up one more time. "Sure big man, cling to your managed way of life. Everything that happens, every angle for you is an angle for the better. That is one fact of Negro life unchanged around you. We cannot take our right to progress for granted. You can, we cannot." Then, folding his hands on his lap Lucas fell silent. He knew they did not want to hear more.

"Souls probing goyem to learn their bowel habits. Racial motivation, persecution, the Ashkenazi fear complex, that sort of thing." Avigdor had been ignored long enough. "My ancient Hebrew soul," raising his arms to the ceiling, still holding his glass, which had a mixture of ouzo, metaxa and cognac, "shekel worshipping landsmen. Money is like a Semite's prick. Today it's in your hand. Tomorrow it's up your arse."

Sam was sputtering with anger. Vania touched his arm to calm him. He looked like he wanted to go after Avigdor. "Have you children?" I asked them, hoping tp break the tension.

Vania, nodding looked at her husband with some alarm.

"We don't ask about your family, don't ask about ours." A hurt grimace locked his thick features for a moment. Then he shook it off, avoiding my question to focus on Avigdor. "The Jewish soul is the only labyrinth of mystery left to man."

"My labyrinth? What an unusual place to dig for traitors, Mr. KGB."

"What an odd Hebrew of Zion you are. Is nothing sacred? What does your life mean?"

"My days are swifter than a weaver's shuttle and are spent without hope," Avigdor said with clear diction despite his drunken condition.

"Damn phlegmatic Sephardi," Sam said.

"You behave more like an Israeli than he does," I told

him. "Your probing, your chauvinistic arguments and concealed motives. You lack only a dark Jew's form and breeding."

"Egomania, false neo-Christians, a passion for iconoclasm, that's the breeding of the lot of you," Big Sam accused.

Avigdor raised his glass to peer at Sam and Vania through the cognac, searching for a phrase. "... that the Jews of Europe worshipped only money as their God, that they were as worthless as fleas humanly — that Jewish religion was contempt for art, history, humanity..."

"That's not in the scriptures," Nancy said.

"Karl Marx, an early dialectic." I explained. "He named it a World Without Jews."

"You give away your scholarship, soldier," Vania said sharply, glaring at me.

"Hey I didn't recite that."

"It effectively made the point," Lucas said, then signaled to Costa for another bottle of cognac. There was a wary moment while Costa was pouring the round into fresh tumblers. It was broken when Don raised his glass to Nancy and said something in Greek to her. She nodded slightly.

I learned later that Don had proposed another shock topic to steer the conversation away from him. It could have been fun, but took a turn that ended badly for me with Nancy.

"Nancy," Don began, "a cracker doll of your nature and talent should know why you work in Piraeus among deviates and prostitutes. Tell us."

She brought the tumbler to her lips, tipping the cognac past her white teeth, holding in her mouth a moment before swalling.

I spoke up suggesting, "She will reply in pornographic poesy to answer you. A search for kindred response, artistic recognition, that sort of thing."

Her reply was simpler, "To eat."

Avigdor laughed and snorted. "Eat what?"

"Life."

"Well put," Vania said.

"Your illicit embraces," Sam asked, "what do they count for?"

Vania answered for her, "Power, warmth, security in a lover's arms."

"No, mam, that's male pressure. I set the rhythm and action."

"When he's finished, how does he treat you?"

"Nothing is finished. We kiss for what we give to the other, and sister it's good."

Sam put his next question to me. "How do you see her with you?"

"Man, I see and I taste with the premier head-giver on the continent."

Nancy looked displeased with that remark. I went on. "There are casual fits of tyranny disguised as whims, capricious humor for self-indulgence meant to hurt a bit. I respond to her the way a man is conditioned to preserve his masculinity."

"You have yourself figured pretty well," Vania said. "Do you have her figured too?"

I shook my head. "Together we make it well. Two peripatetic sex-tramps who collided at the right moment. I will say this though Nancy is the first love-girl in a long time who did not try to sicken me with sex guilt."

Vania looked at Nancy, then at me. "Doubt is the thorn in the America male soul. If you carry guilt it's in the blood. Otherwise you would not be taking it to bed with you."

Nancy puckered up her face and began to sip more cognac, changed her mind and put the tumbler down. "You men, whatever your complexes, have preconceived ideas of what women should offer. Once we bed and suckle you, you want to pass your obligations over to us, condition us to the constructions of male society. We won't be held you know. Infidelity is our cudgel."

Vania picked it up from there. "Expectations are different between women as well as men and women. This rarely gets across to Anglo-Saxons, and converted Semites. Perhaps Avigdor knows." She gripped his wrist and wouldn't let him pull away. "Yes, he does know."

"So do Greeks," Nancy agreed, raising her arms, letting her hair sift through open fingers, caressed her neck and sat up in her chair. I thought for a moment she was going to sing.

"Love is less stable than men believe," Vania said.

"I call it thing, Vania. It's doing the thing. Dogs display their love in the street. Interfere and they get stuck like some long married couple. I get the same feeling as the bitch when a guy assumes I belong to him."

"Perhaps," I said, "perhaps Nancy's love is easier. She doesn't need to have any notion of what it is to be loyal about it. It has taken but a few years from puberty, with some detours and deceptions, to find the form of life best suited for her. If she believes it is necessary to do what she likes then it is.

Nancy does not need me for fulfillment. A wayward bird cannot settle for one lover however much her hunger is fed. Use her, don't try to love her, lose her, but remember her. Lovely free bird." I put one hand on the loose hair spread over her shoulder. She leaned away until my hand slipped off.

Lucas said, "The ancient fault with the thing is less the interpretation than a guilty conception of what it ought to be. Religion can imprison a spirit and feel right in doing so. But for organs to bind two souls, twisting their senses beyond the physical, that is a crime against nature."

Big Sam was impressed. " Well put. You two surprise me. I imagined you more superficial, hardly aware of the any sensibilty beyond yours when pricked with the love thing."

"Typical of the cash-oriented..."

Mr. Rosen interrupted what insult Avigdor was about to lay out. "Now if we enlarge on your peculiar attraction for one another we will be doubly enlightened."

"Some things are better left dark," Lucas said.

"I like that," Vania cut in, "dark things left dark."

"Don't be lewd," Sam-Sam warned his wife.

"It was always necessary for me to do what I like," Nancy whispered.

"The sixth sense in the abysses of female secrecy," Donald said. "Judging parallel standards through feminine intrigue." He toasted her alone. "One meaning for you, another for us. Twisting love to maintain superiority. Or is it only a cry from a woman beaten by life and hungry for love?"

Nancy's seemed puzzled about what Don was telling her.

"You did not have him last month and you may not have

him next month. Where is the meaning there? What will you have when he's gone,?" he asked her.

She looked into Lucas' earnest face with eyes that began to blink from tears. "I will have myself." Then almost inaudible, "I will have myself." She filled her own glass with cognac, put down the bottle, picked it up again, poured some in Vania's glass, put the bottle down and began to drink without waiting for us. She was hunched over looking down at the table, sipping her cognac. Suddenly she stood up, tipping her chair over, "Give me your key."

I took the key from my pocket, handing it to her without a word. She passed behind me going towards the door, pausing to look back at Don and Avigdor, then toward Vania but not to Sam Rosen or me, and went out.

Big Sam and Lucas watched the doorway as if expecting her to come back. The debris on the table bothered me. I motioned for Costa to clear everything away and give me the bill. He righted Nancy's chair and waited for Avigdor to drain the bottle before taking it.

On the bill was the food Vania and Sam-Sam had eaten.

"Take that off our bill," I told Costa. "It's not my task to feed them more than I eat in a week."

Vania took the bill from my hand, glancing briefly at the total before handing it to her husband. "Sam-Sam will put this on his expense account."

"Looks like our gathering is breaking up," Sam Rosen said in a friendly tone. "I want to invite all of you to a party two weeks from tomorrow night. The Swedish Consul is a friend of mine, a past president of the International Lawyers' Society. He is giving a party for the Dutch Ambassador, and asked me to invite as many foreign residents as possible to call around. His name is Svensen, a sympathetic guy, you'll like him. Here is the address, and bring Nancy. There will be a Greek band, good food, all kinds of smoking and no spies or cameras. Dress how you like and bring nothing but yourselves. Confirm with Ambassador Svensen's office, his phone number is on this invitation. Okay, will you come?"

I hunched my shoulders, looking for assent from Don and Avigdor who did not say no, and told Sam-Sam that I thought we would but could not promise.

"Fine, I won't pressure you. How about a final drink to round out the night? No hard feelings over our differences, is there?"

I shook my head, meaning no hard feelings, and no last round for me. "I'm going to her," shook hands with my friends and the Rosens and left.

I walked in the cool night of Plaka for some time before turning up the passageway to my room. Nancy sat up when I lit a candle and put it under the bunk. She was wearing a thick blue knit sweater of mine. I did not look at her while pumping the spirit stove before lighting it.

"I'm sorry if anything I said upset you."

"Leave that! Where are Don and Avigdor?"

"Still with the odd couple, or off to Syntagma Square by now."

"I knew you don't trust me, but I didn't feel that you disrespect me for what I am."

"What are you?" I went to face her at the edge of my bunk. Too much drinking made me as cross as it made her aggressive. I was in no mood to take her temper when she began to berate me.

"Use her! Suffer her, fuck her and turn her out. Are you so poor? Am I worth so little?"

"I did not say that."

"That is what you meant."

"I was not aware that an observation which is obvious could disturb you. Still, it was not meant to hurt you."

"Wasn't it?"

I started to snap off a response but thought better of it and turned away to look out the window. It was easy to see her faults. Who could protect her from them? Not me. No one could order Nancy what to do or what not to do. Probably she searched for something that did not exist, or somebody who would sacrifice his private life for her. Well, that was not me. I took advantage of her vulnerability, her loneliness and need. If I did not watch my temper I would lose her before I found another being to embrace. Her raving from my bunk was like another voice muffled in the clouds scudding the dark sky.

"I don't deny how I am but you sounded pretty cheap saying it."

I did not turn to watch her face, which I was sure had a hurt grimace.

"Vania had the decency to defend me. You mocked me like that hippo mate of hers. To you I'm just a darling alcoholic drinking away the hurt before coming to bed with you."

I turned away from the window, put grounds in water that was boiling on my spirit stove.

"You know my best romancing back home was cheating with married men."

I nodded. "You told me that."

"A married man can't make a tied bitch of me like you would if you got half the chance."

This I answered, telling her that I had no such intention in mind. She dismissed my protest. She had described to me her trysts with married men, banal episodes far below ordinary standards of passion. The pace with which she moved from one city and job to another, from one cheat to another was well documented. In New York: bed partner to her boss, typist for a political columnist in Chicago, traveling secretary with national sales manager in Los Angeles, another in Las Vegas — all bed mates paying a salary. She knew the names of wives, the ages and names of all their kids. I had listened with distaste for what it told me she was.

A puzzling impression set in my tired mind and spread to dim recesses numbed from fatigue and drink. Her manner reflected something about our affair, that it really meant something more than she intended, something unplanned, yet insistent.

"You were right. There is little doing with me. How well you put it to those freaks tonight. Use her! Lose her! But try to remember. Remember what? What you remember about Avigdor's wife? I wish you had gone to Sarai long ago. That's your next fuck stop, isn't it? Avigdor is going to Paris, and you to Israel panting after his wife?"

I stopped making coffee, turning again toward the window to think what to say or do. I had not seen her upset like that before. She murmured a poem which she later wrote out and left for me. Maimed waif of change, her verse as transparent as her attempt to conceal her need for genuine love. She read my thoughts when I turned and came towards her.

Propping herself on one elbow, swinging her head to clear the hair from her face, turning on me with those magnificent troubled eyes, she said, "Cat got your tongue? Afraid to say the wrong thing again? Scared I might leave you? Then what will you do, play with yourself?"

"Most women of your attractiveness are man eaters."

"Am I that?"

"You're a woman eater gnawing at them through their husbands."

Her bitchy reply came sharply. "I wish Avigdor had come here instead of you so I could get at your Sarai."

I went out of my place leaving her to sleep off her temper, or leave.

Bordello

To be keen and controlled, unaffected by feminine wiles, what man is able?

I went directly to the one house in Athens with no male prostitutes. The girls were unusually pretty, none more that sixteen years old. The one I got was surely not over fifteen. I wondered what condition of life directed her to the humiliation whoredom offered. I was with her more than an hour using her wretchedly. Out on the damp street unable to shake off the meanness of the bordello and the child I had mishandled, sister to Nancy left in my poor room, I wondered why I went there. Was I tricking Nancy or myself?

My gloom matched that of the black clouds over the Parthenon. The decayed pagan stones perched on the Acropolis mocked the balls of Church domes, smooth as an alter boy's anus, leaking thin blood. Invaders abused and raped Athenians each millennium to date. What a waste of intelligence and passion. Traditions maligned, belief in myths done for. The cause is too perverse to cure with prayer.

Sodom and a Greek Passion

I stopped in several bars to drink arak. My head was cloudy when I came upon Don and Avigdor in a late night men's bar. They were drinking like conspirators the way Greek companions drink. Avigdor's arm was draped over Lucas' shoulder.

"Hey Spartans, come to terms, have you?"

"With our natures." Lucas led me by the hand to the bar and gave me his drink.

"Dear me Donny, now we are found out. What will our friends think seeing us here together?"

"What else could they think in this queer joint?"

"No bloody fear," I shouted, turning to the guys in the bar. "hear all ignoble chicks with dicks, no incorrect conjectures about Moses Avigdor and sister Lucas."

"Butch," an Oxford kind of accent came from a booth where a thin man was playing with a burly Greek.

Avigdor asked about Nancy. "Did you beat her?"

Lucas accused: "You choked her, cut her up and threw her white breasts to Plaka cats."

This angered me. "Faggoty envy," I screamed at him, cutting my hand when I slammed the glass on the bar. "Bring drinks for us bartender."

"Please quiet your friend. Tourist police will give us trouble if they come."

A young man from down the bar approached me. "Strong, maybe sexual man. Drink with me."

Swinging clumsily at him I fell on my face. Lucas and Avigdor tried to calm me. Raising my glass I brought it down to smash on the bar. Silver slivers tore my flesh. Grabbed by hands gripping my testicles I was tossed into the dirty wet

105

street.

Picked up by my friends, leading me and pulling me, we three wise men took refuge in a dry cathedral. Early Mass was happening intoned by an untidy disciple at the podiou ejaculating holy juice. Voices of choir boys like gelded calves pierced the stale interior.

"I feel so righteous," Avigdor sang out, daring to wobble up front to taste that handled pill and watery wine.

Gigantesque... my head so big, feel so big, cannot get out. Blocked - blocked - BLOCKED! The door high as the wall. Break it down. Hit it, smash it, break Nancy, break my bleeding heart.

Early sun drying us. Crawl steps to cave trap. My Jewish cousin and Black Soul Brother were caressing on my stairs pressing into one another like over-ripe fruit.

I cannot make the stairs. Lucas helping, Avigdor opening my door: "Is she there?"

"Only her smell."

They lift me into my soiled bunk. Then they left me to have at each other in Lucas' place.

Left alone, bruised with split hands, split heart, split woman like a rejected bitch sobbing over eddies of blood, an isolated hulk of human waste, my private hell was sucking me down like love dizzily sinks.

Delphi

Two days following our quarrel that bad night I needed some space between Nancy and myself. She had not come to Plaka since then so I left a note on my table and another note at Taverna Diogenes. I wrote that I was going on a bike tour to Delphi and we should meet on my return within a week

At Delphi the days were fresh with thin rain at the Oracle's dark caves. The grey skies softened the ruins of the arena and temple. The view over the cushion of oliverias spread along the valley to the Bay of Korinthiakos. I biked down treacherous roads to the sea where I stayed three days in a fisherman's beach house built on sand laced with mica. Each evening meal was served with fresh fish cooked by hands scarred from mending fishing nets. My last day there I walked for hours along the shore thinking of Nancy, brooding about our stormy relationship.

The evening when I got back to Athens I went to the taverna. after finding three notes in my room from Nancy, each asking me to find her waiting in the taverna for my return. She was there at our usual table with three men, old Nikos the poet, Yiannis the sailor, and a heavy man in new clothes who combined the air of an army officer with something else, an indefinable sense of knowing the dirtier side of life. He was joking with Nancy about her expired visa telling her that his penalty could be severe or easy depending on how she responded. Then I remembered who he was, the horny Alien Department Inspector who some foreigners paid off with money and sex to extend their visa.

Nancy greeted me quietly with no hint of chagrin, inquiring with what seemed concern about my five-day absence. I touched upon where I had been and how peaceful the land was between Delphi and the sea.

"You said once that we would go there together."

"We still can if there is time before I sail for Israel. Otherwise when I get back."

"Are you still determined to go?"

"Avigdor's family expects me."

"Avigdor left this morning for Paris."

"I thought he was to leave last week."

"He changed his flight for you. He was disappointed because you did not see him off at the airport."

"When he gets home again we will meet there."

"Will you stay in Israel until then?"

"Yes."

"With his wife."

"With Sarai, yes."

Nancy made a grimace and said nothing more.

Yiannis interrupted to remind them of the time.

Nikos and the Inspector were taking Nancy to the

Parthenon becuase the moon was full that night. They asked if I would accompany them. I said I was tired. I wanted Nancy alone with me to talk things over.

Yiannis joked about Nikos' age, hinting of monkey business in the moonshine with Nancy. He recommended the grilled fillet and ordered wine for me. Just before Nancy left with Nikos and the Alien Inspector she leaned over to whisper that she would come to my room about midnight.

While my fish was cooking, Yiannis asked, "Where have you been, we thought you had deserted us? Your girl friend and the Israeli looked for you every night."

"Like your ancient Greek philosophers, I walked the hills between temples."

Shrugging, Yiannis wondered why I let Nancy go with the Alien Inspector and Nikos.

"A night visit up the Acropolis with the ancient poet Nikos, is not an event I need worry about, he's harmless."

"More harmful than harmless," Yiannis said.

"Harmless," I repeated. "The poet will look after her."

"That old pederast will look after her if he can, but not how you imagine."

An imperceptible menace tightened around me.

"Bitch, that old man," Yannis added. When he's finished with her, he might give her to the Inspector and brag about it tomorrow."

I gave my meal over to him and left the taverna.

The moon over Plaka lit the path like early dawn. Ghostly figures walked in the dead shadows of aged pillars shaded grey by the cool light. The inspector was sitting near the south entry to the Parthenon. Nikos and Nancy were not with him.

    I slipped through the temple and out the back court, keeping in the shadow of the temple carefully hunting. Soon I saw them fading out of the moonlight behind a broken wall. Nikos was sifting the fine silk of Nancy's hair through his gnarled fingers. She was leaning against him looking out on the ancient paving, then to the sky, then to Nikos, warming to the thing she was to do. Nikos slowly pressed her head down to the erection between his shaking thighs.

    A thick cloud hung over me as I quit the Acropolis down the back road to Plaka. Chris' sake, what a dirty disappointment. She was giving a blow-job to that old goat. How many others besides Nikos, a man three times her age and a grandfather? Where did the anxiety come from when she saw me earlier? Why did she tell me she would come to my room at midnight if she was first going up there for that?

    Bloody sexual bandit circulating among beleaguered hearts abusing passion to cheat me. Raw independence? Fidelity to an image of herself as free, tilted into something compulsive and illegitimate. Against what should I weigh her morals? Nikos' rogue personality? Yiannis' rough youth? My jealousy? A public act of that sort outlaws those who commit it. It seemed a precipitate and lunatic withdrawal from reason.

    Damn! The strangeness of our situation. What to do about it? Was it my right to do anything? My jealousy seemed so useless and commonplace. Sensual freedom after all, has nothing whatever to do with morals. Nancy and I were not two disparate creatures joined in union for disaster. We were born and deformed in the same land. Even our alienation from America was not too dissimilar. By different paths we had found the same foreign bed. No guilt to shatter us. Even doubt, that Christian crown of thorns, was inappropriate.

Entering my room instead of the taverna, sitting for a while on the one chair at my cracked table it puzzled me that I was not angry. Disappointed, yes, but not surprised that she would do that to the old poet because she liked him. I wanted a controlled temper when she came. I boiled coffee while the spirit stove warmed the room, lit a candle and undressed, then climbed onto the bunk. Despite a long wait my nerves did subside to an edgy semblance of calm.

Peripatetic sex tramp. Did I mean Nancy or myself? Waiting for midnight I tried to make shape of our affair. Our behavior was not motivated by any greedy spirit but by that apparatus sculptured at our centers from birth. My thoughts were unclear, the weight of our absurdities heavy. I almost dozed off when the midnight chimes rang in the city.

A knock on the door. Who? Nancy would simply walk in. It was Donald Lucas.

"Pour yourself some coffee, why the late visit?"

"Nancy."

"What about her."

"Nancy played around while you were away."

"Unfaithful?"

"Yes."

"Should I be surprised about that? I long ago decided not to expect fidelity from a woman when we are only bound sexually."

"Imagine who with."

"The gentle poet Nikos for one. Yiannis no doubt, or maybe you, so what?"

"Guess once more."

"Why should I?"

"It was Sarai's husband, Avigdor."

"What?"

"Yes, Avigdor. They waited here the night he postponed his flight. It happened in this room. Nancy figured it would be some kind of justice should you slip in on the scene unexpectedly."

"All right, I am properly shocked. So why are you telling me this?"

"Masculine reactions intrigue me. Avigdor's that night and yours now."

"Hell of a way to salvage your manhood."

"The fact that he was able to screw her was amazing."

"How do you mean that?"

"He told me he was always impotent with his wife. But he ain't impotent, believe me. His Sarai must be frigid. Your Nancy had no struggle working him up. She knew all the Turkish boy joys in addition to her feminine tricks. She drove our Hebrew wild. When Avi came he shrieked like he was getting a second circumcision. It woke half of Plaka. He stared at his leaky penis like it had never experienced such pleasure until Plaka aroused the same love level that you and Nancy reach."

"Plaka seems to have aroused you and Avigdor more than us. You guys are as alien to Greece as Plato would be on the moon. From the way you describe that zesty scene I suspect you could have been in this room with them."

"My dear Jupiter, I was."

"Lucas, you're high on hash. Get your black ass out

of here. My delinquent is expected any time. Should she find you here she might think that I finally crossed the River Styx to your queer shore."

"Precisely. She should find us whacking off together. It's time for you. Poetic justice, to use her words, and that good stuff."

"Get the hell out of here. You can try her when I go to Israel. Out! Get out! Fuck off."

"All right I'm going. But that horny bitch will eat your heart along with the rest of you."

"Good night sister."

"Mothafucka," he called me and stormed out the door.

I was awake when the door opened with a slight squeak and Nancy slipped inside. She undressed in the cold and climbed up to lie beside me.

"Are you asleep?"

"No."

"I didn't think you were."

"Are you still vexed about my going off to Delphi?"

"Not any more, Mac. Futile for me to have upset myself about you might do."

What I said that night we quarreled merely confirmed what you have been insisting..."

She stopped me with that familiar gesture, placing her fingers on my lips "You and I have had a fair relationship here. Can we keep it like that and not go into past quarrels?"

"Sure, Nancy, why not?"

"Yiannis said that he and Avigdor saw you go into a whore house before you left Athens."

"That night I took another girl."

"Was she good?"

"A child prostitute."

"Damn you, I am not pleased you needed her in place of me."

"You were not neglected during my absence, I am sure."

"I have been waiting in this room or in the taverna. I missed you, you are real good for me. I needed you to recover from the strain of those taverna freaks pawing at me every night. Believe me there is no one better to nourish from than you."

"Yiannis? Nikos?"

"They have been sympathetic and supportive over my concern for you."

"For which the poet was richly rewarded by your pleasing tongue in the shadows of the Parthenon."

Her reaction was a flash of anger that vanished, and resignation that lingered. "Were you up there?"

"I left at once before I blew my mind while you blew his."

"My dear love you had no right — no right."

"Am I your love?"

"More than you can believe."

The candle flame spit reflections on the window. There was a trying silence while she began to caress my flesh. Her touch was pleasant but there was no sexual stirring. My mind turned on to her energy, love's genius within her body. It was anarchic like stray current sensing the onslaught of future loss. I felt anxious at that moment and wished that Nancy were someone else. This permitted me to rationalize how her life, like mine was a life of remote chances, squalid affairs and uncertainty.

We were insecure lovers. Could that be why she let

men take advantage of her? Her vulnerability, her loneliness and need could not conceal her fears. Would she sleep well alone? Or like me was she destined to become victim to empty nights? My mind was fighting against pity that very possibly might be my love for her. "Loss, loss and waste is what we do with ourselves," I told her.

"Of what I do with my own body."

"No, of my dumb resentment — that I should intrude on you and feel anger when you behave exactly like I have with others."

"Is that what you were thinking about?"

"No. This is just what I am saying."

"Are your thoughts turned in on you, or against me?"

"Not against you, Nancy. What I think about your behavior does not change how I feel about you."

Her fingers were touching my hair. "Beautiful what you just said. Don't spoil it by telling me what else was passing through your head. I am psychic you know. I'll surprise you one of these nights. I'll sense when you are willing the opposite to what you say. And it will affirm what we have both denied."

"What is that?"

"What is what?"

"What have we denied?"

"A meaning to what we are about that is deeper than you merely penetrating my several orifices."

I studied her ingenuous posture. She had turned towards the dark window, her eyes searching for something in the bright night. I had never seen her calm like this before, yet alert to what I would say. When I drew her thin fingers to my lips she looked at me. Her jewel green eyes were dark, uncertain, prepared for pain.

The candle hissed softly, flickered and went out sending up a tiny glob of odour and smoke.

"I suppose you are judging me. All right do it. Don't tell me your verdict though."

Wrapping my hand in her soft hair, her tears were warm on my fingers. I waited suspiciously, disbelieving that her emotion was only for me.

"You are good you know. I ask only kindness from you."

"You are reasonably sweet yourself but you ain't no saint."

"No, I sure ain't, and you ain't no saint either. Saints are impossible to live with. Give me a devil like you anytime." She smiled and kissed me. "You okay?"

"Yeah I'm all right now about you with Nikos up there. The concept of love is too deep for our poor minds. We are not equipped to support happiness."

"I don't know about that.. I fit better in life than you think I do. I know life is a cheat. I never truly expect to come out well. I get more satisfaction winning small pleasures than I would if happiness smothered me. You love me I believe, and leave me free. And I love you — I really feel it. There! I said the damn word. It's the first time I ever said this to a man and meant it."

She kneeled over me trying to release my tension, caressing and kissing my flesh, trying to draw tenderness from me. I moved Nancy to bring her alongside me. We held each other closely. In that troubled embrace was forgiveness.

Sounion

Sounion Temple, or what remains of its fallen structure, is on a high plateau at the southern-most point of land on the continent of Europe. Like most of the early temples built in Southern Greece, it is a day's walk from the Parthenon.

Nancy and I decided to hike all night to Legrena a small farming town a mile down from the temple. We were expected before midnight at the house of a Dutch couple. We rode a bus to the outskirts of Athens and started out on foot. It was a wonderful Aegean late winter night, crisp and clear, perfect for such a hike. The sinuous road down the coast, rarely losing sight of the sea., is spectacular. We could sense the spirit of ancient philosophers on the same trail when it was earth and rock.

There are two descending stretches to sea level that rise again at Vouligameri and Avavissos, both tiring to ascend. After the second climb Lagrena was seen in a valley awakening just before dawn. A slight inflammation over the hills cut into the hazy pallor. The sun rose rapidly as if in a hurry to warm us when we got to the house of our friends.

The owner was Baron Hugo de Wilde van Kooiker. His concubine was Ina, a striking Indonesian/Dutch beauty with a child's slim body and anxious eyes. She had been his companion for years, endured a great deal of callousness from him but loved him beyond the sexual.

Ina was twice married, had three beautiful children of mixed parentage, forgot her husbands as soon as she divorced them, her lovers as well. Until she met Hugo, Ina took love so lightly that her manner always retained the restlessness of a single woman.

During our night hike, Nancy and I spoke about them, avoiding our own anxieties. When we got to the house a note explained that Hugo and Ina would return from Corfu in a few days and that we should make ourselves at home. We had a long sleep and a late lunch the next day.

We explored the region between Legrena and Sounion. Our relationship was tranquil, our comportment respectful, our love-making satisfying. It was an artificial calm before I was to leave Nancy for Sarai. My departure date hung over us like a loose branch.

Our final weekend together was the last week of winter. The afternoon was almost spring-like, the cyclamen buds on the cold branches too wary to blossom yet. We started out the next morning for Sounion, hiking up a path on scraggy rock land rising to a wide knoll shaped like a grape leaf where the broken floor of the Temple began. Huge chunks of marble pillars were strewn around the site as though broken by a Cyclops giant. At the high point ending at the cliff's edge it was three hundred feet down to black boulders crowding the watery shore.

Probing waves broke over them, obsessive restless whispers, the oldest continuous sound in the world.

We stood watching the magnificent facade that follows the sun's decent. Nowhere have I been more moved by its beauty than on that ragged land's end. From the platinum line of the sea's horizon a blue haze moved protectively towards the shore. I thought Nancy was seeking comfort when she moved closer to me.

She was holding my hand and asked me not to stay at the edge looking down. "You might push me."

Her fear puzzled me. While hiking up Nancy had been shedding snatches of song like leaves turning in the late breeze. What misgiving had altered her?

I looked at Nancy, affected by the anxiety she transferred to me. I moved back still holding her hand. We pressed against the broken temple wall, her arms gripping me like she had never done before. I opened my coat to pull her close for warmth.

"Desolation."

"What did you say?"

"Desolation makes people lovers; the pressure and fear of loneliness."

"I suspected that about you, Nancy."

"Suspected what?"

"You are afraid of isolation. It blocks the spiritual love that we males yearn for. Our cadavers mesh superbly but we both know the limits. Only sex binds us. And we are helpless against parting."

"I know, I know, and I can't help it."

Kneeling on the hard stone she reached for me under

my coat. I was shaken by her moans like the sad wind. The twilight fumbled its colors leaving the slim crescent moon to watch.

We did not sleep well that night. Lovers under trial of separating use emotive words, exaggerate their meaning. Better nothing said. The awkward silence between us was a truer sentiment. We had the morning left before the Athens bus would come through Lagrena. Nancy would take it alone and thus avoid a sentimental parting at the port.

When she came to the table for breakfast her face was expressionless. She barely ate what I had prepared.

"The way you are watching me is callous."

"Oh?"

"Well, aren't you?"

"Stoic maybe. I am not indifferent about what is happening between us. I suppose what you see is my defence mounting around my heart to ward off repercussions from our love lost. If I let every parting bruise my soul I would be a wreck by now. How do you handle it when a guy goes off?"

"I wish I was that strong. It bruised me every time."

"Well this break-up won't leave bruises. It may be a relief for you to get a guy nearly twice your age out of your hair."

"You are crude and mighty vain, but it was me who chose you that first night in the taverna. I wanted you — still do. Our thing has been wonderful, a happening I will never forget."

"I will not easily forget you either, believe me. We are two of a kind sharing common love worship. We used one another well. Hopeless too but like you said, something not to forget."

"Just the idea of permanence was hopeless. There is nothing I regret. Please believe that."

"Forgive my smile. Its source is malice. Really I weep for what we have lost."

"Gained! We have gained. You understand how we must be free. I belong to no one and you to everyone. You belong to me and to every woman. Universal love covers us both equally. Nothing changed by what we did. To take more from the act would bring more confusion." She rose from her chair to kiss my face and neck.

I could have stopped Nancy there to accuse her of selfishness, to point out that her desire to embrace the sensual world was an infidelity and self-indulgent. Afraid she would mistake how I meant it I said nothing.

So forlorn and used, I thought while her taste overwhelmed me. *Not a free woman at all, just a mere bird of terror. She will be done in. Sure as hell, like all fragile lovers, she will be done in.*

"What kind of man will you want finally, Nancy?"

She took a deep breath, grimacing a little before replying. "I will want a man with gifts not too inferior to yours; a poet with Lucas' sensibility, and a mystic with Avigdor's fanaticism to conclude that life is worth struggling through."

Tilting my head I did not at once reply. I did not want to analyze how I felt then, that perhaps the end of life itself was probably easier to bear than these parting deaths and dreadful resurrections into vacancy and pain. I could not concede to her that I was hurting. "I may be quite wrong, but I believe you want me to leave Greece."

"But you don't think you are wrong, do you?" I looked

up to see if she was mocking me. "As usual you are right." Pausing to raise both hands she barely got out these words that surprised me. "I think want to go with you to Israel."

I was surprised she said that. My reply was a slow shaking of the head.

She went back to her place and sat down slowly, tears washing her eyes. "I am a simple girl with no holy philosophy."

Going to her I tried to comfort her. Then she surprised me again.

"Carry me back to bed. I want you to love me."

We did not speak, watching each other with eyes full of tears. To love her was to hold her. She fell away in a stroke of sleep on my chest. Her face was calm, beautified with an ineluctable appearance of virtue. I was obscured by the idea I had seen her like that before — when she sang in my room that morning in Plaka when we first made love. Before I shut my eyes I heard the horns of the Athens bus announce its arrival in the village. When I woke Nancy was not beside me. My mind did not connect the bus and her absence at first. I went to the terrace and saw her facing the sea.

"I'm sorry you missed your bus."

"I'm not."

"Will you take the night bus?"

"No."

With that answer I thought the block in her feelings had been removed. "Would you like me to stay on in Greece another month?"

Shaking her head she looked at me.

"Do you still want to come with me?"

Her expression lightened a little. "Is that what you

want?"

"I think so but I want you to be sure about it. It might be wiser if I go first. The next boat to Haifa is the second Sunday next month. You can come over on that one. We will be among easier friends there."

"A jealous Sarai, I am sure."

"She would not be jealous."

"I don't know. Sarai may not share you. I might go next month to join you, or I might not."

I was going to say something when she touched my lips to silence me. She sensed my anguish. We had given too much to lesser affairs. Our souls were overworked and could not sprout fresh blossoms of love. We knew it was goodbye.

Sitting together, our breaths on one another, we listened to the cadence of the sea. I raised her hands to the level of my mouth, pressing my lips to her knuckles, looking into those beryl-green eyes with diamond drops of tears. I left her crying when I walked from the house toward the water.

Passing behind Legrena along a trail bordered with scraggy brush I emerged at the shore. Dizzy from the wavering pattern of emotions turning in the Greek air, I could not take in the quality of that morning. I had been wrongly judging our affair, believing that erotic behavior between two like us would have a binding effect, which nothing could upset. Envy for her sexual emancipation gnawed at my groin. Strange reasoning for I was no more bound than she. I did not suppose that the abuse our love created was damaging to her. In some way I hoped that she was tougher and would go on to a better companion than I was.

The sea cursed the shore. I touched it near the base of

the knoll Nancy and I had ascended the day before. But I would not go up there alone to that precipitous point where the cracked terrace trembles at the edge. Her spectre might push me over. The air was scented with a haunting fragrance peculiar to winter's end. In the failing light was created a ragged profile of savage beauty that my mood could not match.

For a moment I thought I understood the appeal Greece held for Nancy. But the idea could not hold. I was too foreign, too satiated and worldly wise, yet lacking the history Greeks honor. My encounters had left me too hard and unfeeling.

Hugo and Ina returned before dusk. The pre-lenten festival was in its last days and the local taverna owner had asked them to come for his party.

"You are coming with us tonight," Ina said.

"Did Nancy accept?"

"Yes. She asked Hugo to go find you. She was afraid you had gone back to Athens. Have you quarrelled?"

"Not exactly. We are victims to the nerve ends of our affair. I leave for Israel soon."

"Is she not going with you?"

"No."

"You can't leave without her, you know. She will be miserable. And you too."

To this I did not reply being full of my own thoughts.

The lone taverna in Lagrena was a squat cement blockhouse with a closed-in terrace. It was reached by crossing a dusty yard. Beyond the terrace was an inner hall with an earth floor. The small dining room was decorated for the feast. Along one wall were long boards holding platters filled with a variety of dishes: tomatoes, cucumbers, feta cheese soaking in olive oil with mint leaves, chickpeas, eggplant, and trays of roasted lamb cuts wrapped in grape leaves.

On a bench next to an old Seeburg jukebox sat two muttering old women with children asleep on their laps. Minding the cash drawer was the tavern owner's mother-in-law who was watching us malevolently.

Jurgos, the taverna owner, a huge friendly man came to meet us, assuring us that the party would be great when the others came. He ordered his small son to bring a litre of retsina whispering to Hugo that it was on him — glancing carefully towards his wife's mother. Except to turn her eyes she had not moved. Gaunt and threatening her lips almost turned in on the dark cavity of her toothless mouth. She knew her daughter's husband had given us something because the boy passed behind her trying to hide what he carried.

The property was from her dead husband, the taverna given in dowry for Jurgos to marry their daughter. An ugly and dumb woman with a dark moustache, she toiled in the kitchen ten hours a day. She could find no husband in the narrow circle of villagers and was nearly thirty when a local sailor, Jurgos, was bribed to marry her. Jurgos was cashiered out of the Greek navy for offensives, abnormal even for them. It was a joke among townsmen that he could manage lovemaking in the dark with his wife, since her moustache gave him the sense she was a male. The results of their copulating was a fine brood of kids with enormous dark eyes.

Family groups from surrounding farms began to arrive. Tables were moved in a long row and our table was joined to them. I felt in no mood to dance but there was no resisting the pull of Greek countrymen. When the older men began to tire, the wives and mothers joined the men making it proper for Ina and Nancy to enter the dancing circle.

In an hour only Nancy and the younger men were still going strong with records from the jukebox. Everyone was delighted with Nancy's skill with the traditional Greek dance patterns which they had learned as children. Her singing of their songs made our foreign presence doubly welcome. I was sure the numerous cognacs that kept arriving at our table were sent so that we would let her be.

Between records, when Nancy was not besieged by admirers, I tried to get her to rest a bit. She shook her head, springing up again at the first notes of the strings.

When she went outside to the toilet shack, Ina told me to follow her to make sure she was not molested. Outside I saw one of the young dancers near the edge of the terrace. When Nancy was coming back he accosted her, placing both hands on her breasts, whispering obscenities. I was about to interfere when Nancy looked at his face, picked away his dark fingers pawing her and shook her head.

He stepped aside to let her pass, hunching his shoulders with that work gesture of southern Europeans that denotes incomprehension.

Ina had danced very little because she was pregnant. Hugo asked if we were ready to leave. I was, but not Nancy.

Watching her moving to the Greek music made me aware of how exciting a physical creature she was. She was the lone huntress and had I not been there she would have chosen a Greek lover for that night.

With so much drink ingested by the guests, I was afraid her provocative behavior would create trouble. I doubted if I could handle even one of those countrymen, much less several. My sense of loss and perhaps jealousy made me forget that no possibility of such trouble existed. The iron law of Greek hospitality to strangers would never condone it.

Most taverna parties break up when plates are tossed on the floor. The women and older men wisely leave. I purposely let the first plate drop, holding it lightly at arm's length while it slipped from my fingers. There was laughter followed by others doing the same. Glasses were next, some tossed carelessly close to the dancers. Two younger drunks upended their table. Nothing is safe as the breaking infects everyone.

I signalled to Hugo, then picked Nancy up under one arm and strode out followed by Ina and Hugo. "*Kali nikta, kali nikta ... jasou, jasou.*"

Nancy did not suspect that our exit was precipitated by me breaking the first dish. Nor did my act of carrying her out annoy her like I expected it would. As soon as we entered our room in Hugo's house she kissed me savagely. Her face had an expression I had not seen before, set on the edge of anger, but still controlled. I dont't think she cared whether I kissed or killed her.

I lay her down close to me, and held her until I fell asleep.

Awakened in the dark by Nancy cursing and sobbing over me, you bastard. I hate you! I hate you" She had thrown the covers on the floor. In the cold room she hissed curses. "You mother-sucking son-of-a-bitch, where do you get your nerve? Before those people you make like you own me. How dare you? I'm not your whore!"

Then except for her rapid breathing, there was silence

from her. I waited for what followed. "I wish you had gone to Sarai long ago. Used me! Used me, you egomaniac son of a bitch! And now you're going away. Well luck to you, you callous prick!" she screamed.

I put my hand over her mouth to smother her shouting. She sunk her teeth to the bone of my forefinger. I jerked her hair hard to get her loose. Blackness smothered her breathing betwen sobs. I swung off the bed to light a candle on the window sill. She would not let me put a sweater over her. I covered myself with one and forced a sweater over her head but could not get her arms inside which were flailing away at me.

"Don't touch me. I despise you. Your insufferable control, your indifference to what I feel. It's beyond you to understand what it's like to be me. You could have liberated me. You want me to feel shame because I perform like a man, loving your body more than mine."

The gist of what was eating her was out. I reminded her of what she always said about the love thing and the hopelessness of permanence with someone. I forcibly threw in how she never called anything meaningful by a name other than thing, how she never cared whether a man remained for a day, a week or a month and how, by her own admission, it was always necessary for her to do everything she wanted. "Fear about a price for love? Freedom has a price too."

"When have you shown any respect for me? Did you ever ask me to come stay with you? Did you seriously ask me to go to Israel with you? It could be the moon if Avigdor's wife is there. You don't give a damn about me. All your wandering fucklusting is an indulgent masturbation, you insincere egoist!"

Her voice spilled out in the cold room like a tiny fist

beating on me. "Bastard, bastard, mother-sucking bastard!"

I pressed her face hard into my chest to stop the cursing and biting. When she stopped I released her.

"I'm going to be sick. Get something," she pleaded..

Ina came into the room, turned on the light and quickly went out for a pan. Returning she pressed a damp cloth over Nancy's brow to hold back her nausea. Nancy did not seem to hear Ina talking to distract her from staring at me with disgust and hatred. She remained withdrawn from Ina's intrusion as though violated and unable to throw off the shock.

I made a signal for Ina to leave us.

"You hurt me, I'm bleeding," Nancy said. A mixture of fear, and puzzlement was in her tone. Contrite savage, blood streaming from her nose, eyes blinking with rage and tears, hair matted over her bare shoulders. I thought she would attack again. But she let me hold the damp cloth under her nose and lay her down under the blankets. I turned off the room lamp leaving only the candle lit. In that soft glow I could see the smears from her eye makeup spoiled with tears, and blood stains above her mouth from pressing her head to my chest when she was biting me. The crimson color of her lips cut across her face like a scar.

Then she saw the bite marks on my chest and my bleeding finger. "You should have stopped me." she reached up to touch my face.

There was a grace of movement in that gesture that was strangely humble yet full of dignity. She was offering compassion by her touch, asking nothing for herself. Nancy who had not sought pity or tenderness from me, did not require either now that the end was near.

Hazard

My room was cleared, the cracked table was bare, my bunk, stripped of its mat and covers, exposed the hard boards for the next occupant. Plaka passages were empty when I descended with my canvas bag holding all I owned. The taxi that Yiannis had dispatched was waiting by the taverna. Taking my bag to put in the trunk of his wrinkled old Buick, the driver motioned me to get in while producing the paper Yiannis had given him with the address of the Dutch Ambassador's villa where the party was scheduled. He drove slowly down to Syntagma square, his taxi's fenders brushing vegetable and fruit displays on the narrow street.

I could not resist turning to look back at the blue and rose tinted houses dotted among the white stones of old Plaka. Skirting the slums, the taxi sped past the tavern where I had been roughly evicted one night and helped to my room by Avigdor and Lucas. A wide boulevard carried us out of Athens to the coastal road towards Sounion. Every driveway toward the water was private with large motor craft anchored in each bay.

Big Sam Rosen had included Nancy with the invitation for the gala evening, but I doubted that she would show up. We knew it would be attended by the diplomatic corps, officers of the ruling Greek clique, and their arms-peddling cohorts. They were a harder lot to plum than my odd friends, but we were curious and accepted. As democratic humans, the Greek Colonels were preposterous, the diplomatic corps pompous and smug. They were the collective face of international authority, menacing like dark clouds in our troubled world.

We turned off the highway some miles beyond the airport and went up a dirt road that wound through sparse woods. The road ended at iron gates. There my driver made a U turn and stopped when a guard waved him away from entering the estate grounds. When I pointed to the trunk for my bag he shook his head mentioning Yiannis. I took it to mean he would get it to him and nodded that I understood. Two chauffeur-driven cars were at the gate waiting for guards to check the occupants. I walked past them, gave my name and was promptly admitted to the grounds.

Thick palm trees lined the path I walked to find the house. I took a wrong turn alongside a languid stream, coming upon the remains of a small temple and the walls of a public house of the classical period. A restored stone wall built by masons in the third century stretched forty meters along a carefully manicured lawn. I felt the force of ages pressing me as though I was walking in a rut of time with both ends dug out.

I doubted my feelings about my comrades who were falling away one by one. Avigdor was already gone, Nancy was no more my lover, and Lucas whom I had not seen for some weeks most likely would not show up at the party. I was wrong there, for Lucas was not one to miss a chance to infiltrate his class enemies despite suspecting that Sam-Sam was Uncle Sam's big eye in Athens.

Dozens of people were on the terrace of the large manor. I recognized the hulks of Sam and Vania Rosen standing near a marble statue. More people were inside the house where every chandelier was lit even though it was still daylight.

For a moment I thought about turning back. The people I approached were not those I would normally seek out for social intercourse. There was no one I recognized besides Vania and Sam. Although I thought the Rosens vicious, there was a human pulse to them. They had convictions. They were understandable.

"Where is Nancy?" Vania asked when I walked up to them.

"No Nancy?" Sam added. "Have you come without her?"

"No. No Nancy," I answered without explaining.

"Your friends are inside, the Greek smuggler and the black guy."

"Mister Lucas, and Yiannis, Sam-Sam. They have names. This is neutral ground here, not Brooklyn Plaka." I had not heard that Yiannis was a smuggler. Why would Sam Rosen know that?

Sam gave his wife an exasperated look, tilting his head and blowing out a puff of cigar smoke before pointing towards the honored guest, Alfred Larsen the Swedish Ambassador.

Larsen was a charming double dealer, a super peddler of war tools to NATO heads with one order book, and the same deadly toys to Warsaw Pact units with a second order book. In addition, he secretly arranged arms shipments to Lebanon for all sides to blow off.

"So glad you could come," his greeting imparting an air of well being I was expected to share. "Heard a bit about you and your Plaka playmates."

"Thanks for including us in your pantomime. When do things heat up?"

"Ah, you know about our evening manners. From which source, Ina and Hugo? Is that why you came, to witness distinguished degenerates at play?"

"Yes to all of your questions — and to participate."

"I like your frankness. It becomes you." Looking beyond me to survey the garden, the ambassador asked, "And your flower child whom Vania described to me with such rapture. Does she share our feelings about pleasure?"

Shrugging I turned to follow Vania, calling back to Larsen that he might get his answer from Nancy herself, if indeed she was coming.

Vania led me to where Lucas was talking with Baron de Wilde van Kooiker, a short, button-nosed butterball with bloodshot blue eyes, doyen of the Athens diplomatic corps.

Madame the Baroness van Kooiker, gaunt and sunken-faced like an Amsterdam whore, was standing behind Lucas slipping her bony fingers down his trousers. Blinking like a turtle she emitted tiny squeaks of joy. Her husband seemed to share her delight in groping Donald's dusty rear end, reaching his hand around Lucas' bum to join hers.

The Baron wore a shapeless purple gown, the same color as his wife's rag. A string of Greek prayer beads hung over his pudgy breast which he fondled with fat fingers, his lacquered nails matching painted toes protruding from his green sandals.

I could picture perverse fantasies torching the brain cells inside his big head when his eyes followed a lithe waiter passing within a foot of his perfumed fat.

Vania restrained him from waddling after the nubile creature by gently pressing her fingers on his crotch, a touch that brought his attention to our presence.

Snatching a tumbler of potent Genever, the dutch gin from his family distillery in Amsterdam, the Baron poured us a round in clay tumblers. His voice, gamey like an old pheasant, spat towards Vania. "Ah Vania, this your other American? His pudgy hand was surprisingly strong when he grabbed mine in greeting. "Pleased you came. What are you doing in Greece? Studying? Teaching? I was told you write. You have a clever air about you, not the lost look of your Plaka expatriates. Bit old for the beat generation though."

I thought, *you smug bastard. Sam-Sam quality nosy and spying, no doubt already briefed about me; same death fat weight like Rosen, same egoism, plus the killer bottle*, then added aloud, "I don't qualify for being of that era. Mine was a generation that beat me."

"Ah," he exclaimed jiggling his tumbler under my nose, spilling his Genever. "Leftist rationale, blame the past and wrong society motives rather than pitch in to help right things, a typical anti-multi-international corporate enemy of world trade, that sort of nonsense."

"Mr. Ambassador, few men know better than you that big business underlies everything in modern life. In the Lord's

Prayer the first petition is for daily bread. No one can worship the corporate god nor love his neighbor on an empty stomach."

"Then you favor cooperate philosophy exporting its superior know-how to the world's less fortunate?"

"Puts precious little food in the mouths of the incurably hungry. Your major business growth is bureaucracy. Your largesse floods the impoverished nations with waste paper, their graves with statistics."

"Informed people are healthy people. Knowledge is wealth."

"The Lord's Prayer is intoned with 56 words. America's Declaration of Independence has 300. The common market directive on the import of groat shoots compiled by the Dutch EEC Commissioner has 29,611 words."

"Well bless me you are well-informed for a retarded flower kid from America the beautiful. What other matter lies close to your heart?"

"Where your treasure is there shall your heart be also."

"What biblical book is that from? Genesis?"

"The Greek chronicle of clowns," I said, sizing up the swelling crowd. "A lot of clowns in uniform at this circus."

"Clever Yank," the Baron said to the Rosens. "We could use him on our side if he could alter his political persuasions." Then in a hoarse whisper he warned me, "move carefully among the clowns and behave yourself. Hold those sentiments about democracy and freedom, or the lack of them under this government. The Officer cadre of Greek Colonels would fail to grasp your humor."

"I will watch out for them, be sure of that."

"And they will watch you."

I was about to respond with something clever but the Baron had already tuned me out, directing his attention towards Lucas' crotch.

"And our darker American here, adding a bit of color to the gathering. No pun intended you understand."

"I understand you well enough," Don said while lifting the ambassador's paws off his brown bum.

I left them to saunter through the main salon. Other than Lucas, the Rosens and myself, there were two guests who did not fit socially. One was a prosperous panderer from Piraeus, the owner of a string of hoyden houses. He bought and sold kids like one would traffic in chickens. This whoremaster was wearing a gold watch on one wrist, heavy gold bracelets on the other, three gold rings and a sapphire cross. Each small finger had inch-long fingernails.

The other man who seemed out of place was about thirty, tall and fit with blue eyes and the fresh complexion that often goes with ginger hair. He had no tan, which marked him as a new man to the city. Intelligence agent flashed from each powered pore. I avoided contact with both of them.

Ina and Hugo, fresh and clean, as though they had just bathed together were descending the marble staircase from the upper floor.

Madame van Elfin tripped rushing by me to get to Ina and Hugo. Hugo picked her up, nodded to his wife, and carried the lady through the crowd. Across the foyer, the poet Nikos was emerging from the music room with the Alien Department Inspector. Thoughts of Nancy with him assailed me. Sighting old Nikos hobbling toward me, age honoring his wrinkly face, an Acropolis shadow passed between us trapping Nancy's long hair in his withered loins. I shook off that image and wondered how that doddering old poet could still get it up. Coming to embrace me, he resembled a saint in the cathedral window. I harbored no animosity because Nancy had used him. He was a beautiful elder, a true philosopher with a shrewd mind who was not afraid to detail in poet's words the tragedy of junta bestiality. He wept daily for the intellectual dissenters chained in island prisons, or released to hobble on limbs maimed by torture inflicted by louts trained in the junta's military.

In every moral sense, Nikos was the antithesis of the Army Colonel and the Alien Department Inspector watching Nikos cross the room. Colonel Georges Kotopoulos, the Interior Minister was a former major of the palace guard. His office was charged with rooting out and destroying opposition to the junta's dictates. A stout brutish man he stood rocking on the balls of his boots looking over the guests with half closed eyes. His dress: black nylon shirt, yellow vest with a silk smoking jacket, was not what one would expect though it did not diminish his menacing aura. He held a pipe and spoke his English with an accent which suggested that if his schooling was not in England his tutor was certainly British. It was known that he had jailed his own daughter and two young nephews demonstrating against the regime inside Athens university grounds. When his brother protested, Colonel Kotopoulos sent them all to the prison camp on Maronisos Island where the nephews were forced to watch their father beaten daily. The camp commander raped his daughter.

Ambassador Larsen was telling me this when his wife and mother-in-law approached. Conversation was mostly in English, not out of deference to me, but because English was the tongue almost everyone had in common much to the chagrin of his wife's mother who liked to think French would be better for the world. Madame Larsen, a small neat woman of unusual beauty, lean cheeks, smooth temples, fine silvery hair topping her skinny body, had that beguiling essence, a way of pouting her lips and thrusting her pelvis which made one think of sex. Chosen friends whom she would service during the course of such parties appreciated her tastes.

Her mother was even more notorious. An ageless sprite, she could not look steadily at one's eyes while talking, because a nervous twitch tilted her head downward, enabling her to study the bulges at male crotches. The mother was the night force behind these high level orgies.

"Alfred darling, are you upsetting this pretty man with your amoral wit?"

"Mankind, mater, we were dissecting mankind."

"Ooh, I would like to dissect this man, or any man, I'm so damn horny." Old Lady Larsen seemed to lose her train of thought. Her nostrils twitched beneath watery eyes, folded hands shaking over her sunken pelvis, her head twisting to follow the movements of firm bums on passing Greek waiters.

The dining room doors slid open revealing a long table on marble pedestals holding rare Greek sculpture from the excavations out back. Aromatic food on silver platters crowded by bottles of Metaxa and vintage wines attracted the hungry. Steaming plates of lamb and eggplant, rice, okra, chickpeas, sesame spreads, parsley, pomegranate seeds, tomatoes, goat cheese and flat loaves of bread were served by youths in green jackets and tight white pants. On the dining room terrace fiery spits were turning whole lambs.

The tall ginger-haired man was in conversation with the Chief of Special Police responsible for security around the house. They both watched me when I walked over the terrace to join Sam Rosen standing with Lucas and Yiannis. Baron van Kooiker was ten metres away with Ina in the midst of armed field officers and the Interior Minister.

Snapping his fingers, the Minister summoned two waiters who served our group with Metaxa.

Toasts were offered. It was tacitly understood that glass tossing was inappropriate since we were drinking from the Ambassador's Czech crystal. But Yiannis upset that taboo.

"To the saviours of Greece, our army of Colonels."

The uniformed men raised their glasses. Others hesitated including the Colonel and the Baron. They stared at Yiannis searching the meaning behind his toast.

Smiling, Yiannis inclined his head in their direction and added, "... the royal family and his loyal subjects."

Everyone now had to join the toast and drink to the very forces smothering earth's oldest democracy. And we all had to toss the crystal glasses on the stone terrace because a toast to royalty can only be offered once from the same glass.

It might have been unpleasant for Yiannis had not Larsen, with a conspiratorial gesture, beckoned Yiannis to follow him outside.

Attention then focused on me.

"What are you doing in our country?" the Minister asked, looking at Sam Rosen, expecting him to answer for me.

"Walking old roads from temple to temple like Socrates and your early philosophers."

"Where do you walk?"

"Through dying villages where old men and frightened women worry whether or not they should communicate with this stranger and inquire what I am doing here."

Big Sam and even the Baron began to smile, then cut it short. The Alien Inspector growled something in Greek to the Minister, then asked accusingly to me, "... You talk politics with the villagers?"

"And history, religion and love."

"What do you hear and see?"

"Mirrors, mirrors like I have seen in other poor places. Fragmented reflections of human conflict. Dramas, betrayals and celebrations."

"What betrayals?" The man with light hair softly asked.

Turning to him, but talking to the Minister I continued, "The saddest thing about military state rule is not the conformity you enforce, but the way you contrive to nullify dissenting voices, even to the extreme of cutting out a man's tongue before you crush his balls."

"No one prevents you from sounding off."

"My dollar-green passport assures me that right."

"Only when your expressions keep within our law. Slandering the Greek state has certain penalties, even for foreigners with your passport."

"I am clean and pure as your heroes," I told him, nodding towards the officers, "and respond to the same lusts," waving my arms towards the debauchery taking place in each corner of the mansion.

"It appears," Fat Sam cut in, "that you accuse the Greek administration of fostering immorality," clearly enunciating the wicked noun so that the military mafia got the accusation.

Pausing before risking a response, I took a glass from someone, sipping whatever it contained while my inquisitors fidgeted. "I may be quite wrong," I began.

"But you don't think you are wrong, do you?" Baron van Kooiker put to me shrewdly.

I went on, "I see no reason in morality why government should not have as one of its intentions the arousal of its citizen's passions. It is one of the effects, perhaps one of the functions of government to arouse lustful desire and I can cite no grounds for believing that the joys vice offers should not be among the objects of desire which government offers along with priests, God, death, widows and strong leaders." My last reference was pointedly directed to the Colonel.

"That reads like something from an old Hellenic drama."

"Every Greek drama is old."

"What you are preaching is heretical nonsense," pronounced the Baron.

"Sociological nonsense," Rosen added.

"The nonsense of any government," I accused, "that has no clear vision beyond keeping in power, fumbling and muddling to develop a strategy to cope with crisis after crisis."

The Alien Inspector held up his hand to stop me going on, turning his head toward the tall ginger-haired man who had a faint amused look that only I seemed to notice.

"What happens to radicals like this in your country?

Have you no means to put them away?"

Shaking his head slowly, the man told the Inspector, "He keeps clear of the violent fringe or we would contrive a conspiracy of one kind or another to charge him. But he wears socks, sometimes cuts his hair, and treads a wavering liberal ideology."

"What political party is that?"

Answering for the agent I said, "Clusters of folk with ideology but without guns are liberals. Thugs with guns but no principles are bandits." Then unwisely, I deliberately focused on the service revolvers worn by the uniformed officers.

Silence splashed among us like damp fog on chattering magpies.

Fate intervened at that tense moment. Ina cut the tension with a pelvic move on the Colonel, urging him to share the pitcher of liquid that she then passed among his fellow officers.

But I was not finished. Thinking quickly how to get myself out of what was clearly a situation fraught with danger, I turned to the tall American. "The fact is, I think, that in Greece we Americans notice a characteristic lack of theoretical issues. Back home we put a lot of pressure on subjects we discuss without threats to each other. Dictators apparently find that embarrassing, if not downright intolerable."

"I find you intolerable," Sam Rosen said.

"Then you and the Baron should not have set me up among these puritans."

"How do you mean that?" the tall Yank asked., frowning.

"I mean that these un-elected Colonels ruling Greece,

whom your White House sponsors, are not unlike you and me: men with convictions of destiny. Minister Kotopoulos here, his life style like his thinking is plain, consistent and puritanical. He and the uniforms are fascist clones who feel a profound sense of responsibility to their own conscience. That places you, sir," turning to the Minister, "in the front rank of puritanism with the king himself. We part company in our means of imparting ideas to less informed mortals."

"Do you fault our methods of discipline?" the Interior Minister questioned with considerable menace, his garlic trace spitting up to my chin.

The Colonel flicked up his hand to shut the Minister off. "Our peasants are not intellects. They are controlled, like you control children to protect them from what they should not know. Dissenters are separated from society to prevent them from fomenting agitation among those you describe as less informed mortals. There are no firing squads, no death chambers, no mass graves in our rehabilitation camps."

"Well, you don't publicly de-ball, or draw and quarter a victim that we know of. Your torture is clinical and curative, you believe. But there are crimes meaner than spilt blood, crimes of character that your philosophers have bellowed against for three-thousand years."

The Colonel, partly distracted by Ina rubbing his medals with one breast while she poured punch over his lips and chin, put her aside, coughing punch spray on her hair. He confronted me with anger so mean that he reached for his pistol. The Interior Minister and Sam Rosen were grinning, nastily pleased that I had really angered the Colonel.

The Dutch Ambassador smirked knowing I was in for

it.

Sam Rosen gasped. "Now you've done it you schmuck."

Uncle Sam's agent was shaking his head. "What a jerk."

The lot of them began to form a ring around me to prevent me from skipping away.

Just then, the Colonel stopped reaching for his revolver, did a half turn and squatted, his tongue wagging at crotch level on the Minister's fly, while reaching out to grip Sam Rosen's sagging rump with one hand and caressing the testicles of one of the waiters with his other hand.

The Interior Minister had a joyful smirk on his face when Ina leaped onto his waist baring her thighs. The Dutch Baron dropped to his knees to suck Ina's toes. Shrieking, she swung off the Minister, pivoting her hips to bowl over the Baron.

Big Sam, picking a waiter up like a baby, cupped him to his soft breast and waddled through the room to the darkening garden.

The Piraeus panderer led three sweet girls and two handsome boys towards the officers. They grabbed their choice, swung them around their necks and headed upstairs, the exposed buttocks of their chattel burping pungent odors.

Larsen returned from the garden without Lucas and led me away. "Stop goading those officers, and show no displeasure if you see one of your friends coerced into a stressful position. Arrest has been ordered for you and Lucas when you leave this property. I have arranged for you, the sailor and your black friend to get away safely. Leave by the garden at ten o'clock. When you encounter a guard, wait for him to say the path is free. Don't mess up what he directs."

With a smile Larsen lowered his zipper and skipped across the room to mix with a score of guests working themselves into passionate hysteria to the beat of eastern music.

The musicians played serenely, heads bent to their instruments diverting their eyes from the sweating creatures engaging in orifice probing with assorted instruments until pleasure moans descended into painful cries while they kicked, bit and spat on one another. Exhausted and pacified the orgy subsided, its players squirming feebly in a pile like a squad of worms.

Returning to the main room I observed the Baron crawling up the staircase, his Genever spilling on the rich carpet leaving its trail of pee color after him. He banged his head on a door that opened, for a naked Sammy Rosen and the Colonel to reach out and drag him inside.

Under the lace covering of the hall table several pairs of bare feet were juggling. Waiters were lined along the wall to take their turn with Madame Larsen.

Mother Larsen was kneeling by the table's edge checking each waiter's state of readiness before she passed them under and into her daughter.

A high scream erupted from behind the gold threaded drapes by the french windows to my left, then a stream of Dutch curses. "Not with that, you pervert!" A male wearing only tie and socks, his features twisted with pain, emerged on tiptoe from the alcove his balls firmly gripped in the painted fingers of Ina's hand. With a final jerk on his testicles, Ina let him go.

Seeing me she ran up to snatch the drink I held.

"The Bastard. He's not even Greek. Don't say anything about this to Hugo. He beats me good when I share my goodies publicly."

"You love it when he spanks you. I should tell him."

"Fucker."

"Never mind, I won't tell. What the hell has got into everybody? They are behaving like virgins caressing their first crotch. And give me back my drink."

"Don't you know? Didn't Don or Hugo warn you not to drink the punch?"

"Nope, why?"

"It's potent, gin, wine, ouzo, my pee and lemon juice spiked with LSD."

"Christ. So that's why everybody got weird suddenly. The Colonel's mafia will crucify us when they recover."

"You'll be gone by then."

"How? There are police thugs all over the grounds. No one leaves easily."

"They will be distracted."

"You can't take them all on."

"Hugo says their first love is money. Women come next. Larsen bought them off."

"He better have or you're done for."

Hugo burst into the room to grab Ina by the hair, smacking her ass before dragging her away.

Looking around I wondered what activity to engage in when a voice alongside startled me.

"Would you like a smoke?"

It was the all-American agent.

"No thanks, I don't smoke."

"Mighty strange goings on here. Never seen the likes before."

"I have but only when LSD floats in their drinks."

"You use it?"

"Nope. You?"

"I carry samples to arouse conversation."

"This pot of horny bodies is well aroused. Not you though. Other than chasing the Dutch beauty you have behaved as well as me."

"Ina was the chaser but Hugo rescued me from sinning with her. I have been watching you. You are the soberest man here, and thus far have avoided the foul play."

"I am careful about what goes into my stomach and where I put my fixture."

"What do you do for amusement, if I may ask?"

"You may ask but I may not tell."

"That your answer?"

"Yep, the same answer for all agent-persons."

"Who do you reckon are agents?"

"You for one and big Sam Rosen for another."

"You are observant. Suspiciously so."

"You bet I am, and observant enough to note how you never take your eyes off Lucas and me."

"Mighty correct. I do this to keep you out of trouble. There are mean state agents around, nasty thought control types dangerous to cross. They neither understand nor tolerate American freedom of speech. Take the Captain who stood behind Colonel Kotopoulos. He gets the political suspects for questioning. When he was a grammar school principal, his method of control was to beat pupils bloody when they talked back or complained. The mothers stormed the school driving him out of town. He cropped up next as the interrogation chief for the Athens junta. Suspects were brought to his office by threes. The first to look at him with any defiance was pitched from a fifth floor window. The other two told him anything he wanted to know after that. The result was more alleged dissenters to imprison."

"Is his file alongside mine at your embassy?"

"Stop talking like a jerk. We have nothing on you."

"Why would you have?"

"I said you are clean. If you were not, the Captain could have you." He looked around casually to note if anyone was listening. "A word of advice if you'll take it."

"I might, what advice?"

"Don't leave here alone. Stay close to your Plaka bunch. And most important, don't take the boat to Israel tomorrow. Don't even go to the port."

Well, I was beyond being surprised about what people knew about me. How could he know I was to embark for Israel the next day?

"Why are you telling me this?"

"Like I said, we have nothing against you. Frankly I don't rightly have to warn you. Might be 'cause you're smart, you aren't queer and don't dope or traffic like Yiannis and Lucas. Can't rightly figure why they are your friends. Your girlfriend is a bit silly, sluttish even, but we have nothing on her either."

"Nancy?"

"The Carter girl. Upstairs here before you arrived."

My eyes looked up the staircase to the first door where I saw naked Sam-Sam enter. "There?"

He shrugged. "Drunk like a country whore."

Just then, as though mentioning her name had sprung her, Nancy came skipping barefoot down the staircase, her thin smock torn to her waist, a lunatic expression on her handsome face.

"Eee ha — zoo-sooie, you fukin' animals. Noah's pimps, two rats," looking down at me and the agent, "pair of snakes," Addressed to Vania and the Baroness, "Rabbits, old birds, beasts and bitches, dalmatians and Danes, Dutchies and Swedes, goys and floys and bitches and boys, that's what van Elphin's orgies are made with."

The Colonel stumbled down the steps to roll beside Nancy who sat on his face. Sam Rosen next stumbled out. Vania came staggering up to me.

"That butcher will kill her. Get her away from them."

The agent-man left my side to rescue Nancy.

"Go help Nancy," Vania insisted.

"Let super-America deal with her." I could not tell Vania that things were being worked out for us to get away from there. I supposed that Nancy was also included in our getaway.

Vania waddled up the stairs to drape herself over the bulk of her husband, trapping the Colonel beneath both of them.

In need of fresh air the Baroness and I walked out to the front garden towards the fountain. A muscular man carrying a jug in his rugged hands approached us. "American you drink. Makes the worries go down."

Chist, is that the spiked punch he's spilling on me? "No thank you. I have enough to worry about without fogging my head with that pissy stuff."

Sodom and a Greek Passion

"I am yard chief. I say you drink with me."

He took a long spilling some over his chin onto his hairy neck. "Have worry you don't drink like friend. You go to jail with the African and dirty girl. No path free, you damn American, no path free."

"Damn? Is this the man with the passwords Larsen told me to expect? Path is free is what he should have said. Too drunk or what?" Looking at the Baroness for confirmation I got no reaction. Apparently she knew nothing about what Larsen had arranged to get Don, Yiannis and me off the grounds.

Holding the pitcher before my nose the yard chief again insisted that I drink. "Not go if you not drink with me. You talk against my Colonel. He kill you if ambassador not stop him. Watch you don't stay in garden when dark."

I had to know if he was the right man to point our way safely. "Why are you telling me this?"

"Why? For thousand drachmas you pay me. And drink that path is free."

I let out a whistling breath. "Wait here, I'll get some more punch and your thousand drachmas. The Baroness will amuse you till I come back, won't you Madame?"

Nodding, Lady Larsen led him to the bushes between trees at the garden fringe.

Inside the room, Ambassador Larsen was watching the episode. Leading me into the music room he asked what was said by the guard.

"He's abusive and drunk. Still he uses free path hints, but has it twisted. He asked for a thousand drachmas and demanded I drink that the path is free. His exact words. Path

150

is free."

"Not good enough. His security chief knows exactly what to say to you, and only to you. Give him this thousand drachmas then come back. At ten precisely it will be dark enough. The yard gang chief will be waiting by the fountain. He will waste no time telling you the right pass words. You must move out with him. He will ask you for nothing. He is well taken care of with promise of double when you have safely gone."

"Okay, I'll feed this gorilla the spiked punch and get away from him."

"Not a guarantee he won't be out there later." Larsen pulled a gold snuff box from his waistcoat pocket. Pouring the powdered content into his glass he handed it to me to fill with punch. Drink to his mother's health with this goblet of punch. Watch until he passes out then come back inside until ten o'clock."

"Is Nancy in shape to leave?"

"She doesn't go with you."

"When the Minister learns we got away he can take it out on her."

"He has taken all he will get from her. The American is a CIA agent attached to NATO in Athens. He's with the oficers now trying to perusade them to release her to him."

"Damn it, I'm sorry to have seen her the way she was for the last time, but glad that she is escaping these military morons."

Madame the Baroness de Smyth van Kooiker and the menace were easy to find in the bushes by the groans belching up from the man. While we adjusted his trousers he happily

Sodom and a Greek Passion

gulped the potent punch and the mickey, while toasting his Colonel, his mother, the German queen of Greece, and anything else he would accept. The thousand drachmas I was to give him went into my pocket when he passed out.

He was lying in the same place when Lucas and I followed the bribed police boss to a hole in the stone wall where the path ran alongside a stagnant stream.

Yiannis had not come at the appointed time. Don and I had no choice but to leave without him.

There was no moon, but bright stars helped guide our way between rocky knolls dusty with flint stone. Descending an arid slope we saw a shallow depression with a pool of water. Yiannis was squatting at the pool's edge. He stood up holding something he took from the body lying still in the water. It lay face up, its calm face powered with the fine silt that covered his eye sockets. The mouth was open like it was going to ask, would you like a smoke?" The tall agent still wore the tie and jacket that made me suspect he was CIA.

Two hours later we emerged at a small orchard with a dim light flickering in the window of a stone house. Holding up one hand to silence us, Yiannis walked to within several paces of the door and whistled. An old woman came out with a lantern. I could see every line in her wrinkled when she walked past Yiannis to stare closely at me and Lucas face. Nodding, she turned back to the house.

Yiannis cautioned us to silence. The place looked unfriendly. I was apprehensive that we were being coaxed into a trap. Finally a strong old man appeared, beckoning for Yiannis to follow him around the house. Ten minutes later Yiannis returned. He was told that the risk of going on through the

152

night was worse than staying there.

We were fed bread and soup and shown the corner where we would sleep on straw bedding covered by goatskin. Yiannis and the old man were talking when I fell off to sleep. My last thought was about Nancy. What happened to her if the agent who was to rescue her was dead in the shallow pool we passed?

Early the next morning we were fed black coffee and bread before being taken to a dirt road where a covered truck was waiting. After riding an hour the truck stopped. I was told by Yiannis to make my way up the trail to Sounion Temple and watch for his schooner. Lucas would go with him. High tide would come in four hours. When I saw a dinghy launched I was to descend to the water.

The day was cool and bright when I hiked up to the remnants of Sounion Temple by the same route Nancy and I had taken. At the top I sat down by a broken column. The sky was a cold blue. The sea, smooth as purgatory, was disturbed by a steamer's prow curling white foam in the green carpet. It ship to Rhodes, Cyprus and Haifa. I should have sailed with it. Instead I was trapped between her and the universe. I was awed by the immense and deliberate art that shaped the scene.

"All the work of God." Nancy once said when we were up there together. Whose God did she credit? At sea the compliment is wrought with an inflexible order that is chilling. It brings to the subject the illusion of a great innovator, dismissing the pagen origin of how it came to be, submitting instead to Judiac and Jesuit thinking dating only to the fifth century before the Christian era.

Its effect did not lead me to praise a prophet's handwork, but to shame me into a fresh realization of how awkward the contrived vessel moving within it was, and how puny I was watching the universe move.

From my jacket pocket I drew out a notebook with Nancy's poetry. Her verses raged at me shook like tiny fists. A part of my strength that had decayed like this temple compelled me to read them for the last time.

> *I could bear my aloneness*
> *And days that limp on broken wings,*
> *A weary body and hungering heart*
> *And the unchanging want of you*
> *If I could make a single sound*
> *Softly and as full of love,*
> *As hushed and calm as your whisper*
> *on a winter night.*

I sighed reading them in her hand writing.

> *Till now I dared not of man*
> *ask any gift from him,*
> *or gentle task of lovers sure promise,*
> *nor refuse what I could give, or you ask.*
> *Love have pity on us both.*
> *Hold tight on this ridge*
> *dividing love from hell.*

I dropped her poor poems down to the sea, the pages brushing the rocky cliff to their cold death. We feigned love to evade love. That day over Sounion, between earth and sky there was space and emptiness and not a promise anywhere.

*　*　*

It is nearing spring on the Fox River where I am watching my infant son asleep before the fireplace. Does he sense the absence of a mother? Will it matter who gave birth to him? How diferent was she from Nancy, or Sarai? My memory recalls the past in disorderly sequence. I cannot hear one echo urging me to spare him what was endured during my life before him. I will bequeath him my prejudices, the wrong kind of stubborn intelligence and a tilted view about women.

Children get the the fathers they deserve.

I had always worried more about about my conquests than my worth. Out of love I was seldom calm, searching and coaxing myself into one untidy bed after another. I recognized the demons haunting me: the panic of failure, a leaning towards perversity. I feared losing control of the mercurial balance between being loved and unworty when I felt unwanted.

If my trusting son was not here with me, these old memories would force me to the woods and bind me to earth's bones until rain and weather rotted my soul.

Haifa

In the fishing hamlet below Sounion where I descended to board the dinghy were silent fishermen who ignored me. They were the only Greeks I had ever seen who were indifferent to a stranger. For them I could have been invisible.

Clouds had filled the sky and it was pitch dark when I climbed onto Yiannis' boat anchored off shore. Only two crewmen were aboard. Lucas was not. Yiannis explained that Don might join us in Rhodos. At midnight I was told to take a turn at the wheel of Sunar. The ship rose and fell gracefully under sail, spray sluicing over the closed hatches. A plume of white foam spread out from the stern like a piece of lace. Yiannis came up to correct my course. He spent some time at the chart table making his calculations for the voyage. When Yiannis had first said that he had a boat I pictured some sort of motorized pleasure craft. The Sunar was a fifteen meter two masted schooner with a teak deck. The cockpit was highly refined with colored power switches, depth sounder gauges, radio telephone and radar that added a new dimension to the craft and its illegal use. I was directed to follow a south east course and was relieved before dawn. Wind whipping the sails and the hull's dance with the waves were the sounds I heard when I fell asleep in my bunk.

We sailed with a strong wind the next day keeping at least a mile leeward of various islands. By then I was keeping the ship on course without difficulty. Again relieved before daybreak, I slept all day, waking about twilight when the ship was motionless. There was a smell of fish, fuel oil and the noise of a winch. Shrill cries of seabirds fighting for offal greeted me when I went on deck.

We were tied to a decrepit wharf at the edge of a small hamlet. There was one dim bulb under a swinging reflector at the far end of the quay. Two men suddenly appeared under the light walking slowly toward the boat. "Don't talk English," Yiannis cautioned. "These are Turkish police."

He invited them aboard. The first man was about forty, as tall as me but broader with a hard face, scarred nose and cheek, dark eyes and curly hair sticking out beneath a knit cap. His hands were tough like leather when he gripped mine. The second man was older, perhaps sixty, slimmer and taller than his partner. He carried a bulky satchel.

Yiannis said that I should remain on deck and followed the two police into the pilothouse. I could see them talking before exchanging the satchel for an envelope. They left without looking at me.

We cast off and headed into open water after they left the dock. "What was that all about?"

"Usual procedure. A contribution to avoid scrutiny of my forward hold."

"Carrying what?"

"Swedish toys consigned to Lebanon."

"From Ambassador Larsen?"

"In league with other perverse diplomats."

"Is Lucas involved?"

"Liaison for them with the Turks. He was in foreign service here."

"I know. Where is he now?"

"Not sure. He should meet us in Rhodos before we sail to Lebanon."

"Is he in that deep?"

"Hasn't he told you?"

"No."

"Better he did not let you in on this. I think he wanted to protect you. The Swede set up our escape because the CIA and Greek Colonels were getting close to busting our gun running. When we dock in Rhodos you will have a Swedish identity. In Cyprus I'll put you ashore about five miles from Famagusta."

We were interrupted by a crewman shouting. In the choppy water a hundred metres to starboard was a slim power boat with four men waving rifles racing towards us.

"Who are they?"

"Water bandits. When customs get their payoff, they tip off these guys. I lost a cargo to them once. It won't happen this time."

"What are you going to do?"

"Watch me."

He took over the controls, increased engine speed when the motorboat neared our bow, then opened full throttle and sliced the craft in half.

We rode the rest of the day and night under full sail to Rhodos where we anchored off shore. Yiannis and one crewman took the dinghy, returning two hours later. Yiannis seemed on edge so I did not ask what came next. The mate told me that Lucas and another man would come aboard in Cyprus. Yiannis later explained to me that my presence on board risked their venture.

"I am going to put you ashore at a cove in Cyprus where someone will keep you overnight. Then you must take a taxi across the island to Famagusta where the regular ferry boat embarks for Haifa."

I did not question what made this plan necessary. In fact I was relieved to be leaving the schooner with its harmful cargo.

Approaching Cyprus Island I could see goats rise on their hind legs to nibble the olive leaves. Twenty small fishing boats were beached at low tide.

We dropped anchor in a cove at the northwest tip of the island. I was told to take a dinghy to shore, drag it out of water and leave it there. Then I was to look for a path marked by a rock cone and continue through an orchard where a man would meet me and take me to shelter that night.

The wind had come up with the tide and four foot swells pushed me swiftly land. I had to drag the dinghy out of the water further down the beach than I expected and did not see any stone cone marking a path. There was a rocky point about fifty meters down the shore so I headed there. A series of niches that seemed cut by man rather than erosion went up the crest of the rocks. I used them to climb about four metres to a flat rock where a small opening made me curious. Squeezing through I went cautiously along a narrow tunnel to where a heavy wooden door blocked the way. Tugging on it was a mistake for I barely was able to jump aside when it came off its rusty hinges. Crawling forward I looked down into a pool with daylight coming from a small opening. A ledge followed the curve of the pool chamber to another opening opposite from where I was. My instinct was to back out of there the same way I came in.

But my curiosity drove me to crawl around the ledge till it ended at a gap with another wooden door. This one I carefully pulled open and peered inside. Light came from two openings in the roof that was formed by natural rock. Stacked on rough plank shelving were pressed bars of a dark substance wrapped in oiled paper. A table held a partly packed box of the bars. I had come upon a hidden store of hashish.

I was not about to touch that stuff and decided to clear out of there pronto. I climbed to the opening in the cave roof and was about to squeeze through when I heard voices. Carefully raising my head I saw a launch with four men approaching the beach where I had dragged the dinghy ashore.

Figuring they could not reach the high point of this knoll from outside, I squeezed through the opening and quickly made my way down to thick brush for concealment

Because dusk was approaching, I thought it best to lie low. My only hope was that the four men would not believe that whoever left the dinghy on shore had been inside the hash cache. About an hour into darkness, I got up and tried to find a path where prickly bushes would not sting me too much. Where the land rose sharply I ascended in order to get my bearings to determine which direction to walk the next morning. Polaris was bright in the north heavens telling me that I was rightly heading south.

When I got to the top my senses tightened, cautioning me that something was not right. A voice spoke softly, "I am a friend, say nothing." In the black shadow the figure looked like a giant. "Are you lost?"

"Yes," I whispered too surprised to react otherwise.

"Are you alone?"

"Yes."

"Who are you hiding from?"

"I don't know."

"Did four men land in a boat after you did?"

"Yeah, I think so."

"Why?"

"I'm not sure. I came upon a cave of some sort and when I saw the men come ashore I got out of there."

"The boat you came from. Do you smuggle with them."

"Absolutely not." I was sure he would ask next why I left Yiannis' boat alone in a dinghy.

Instead, he merely said, "Then I will help you, come." He led me a motorbike lying on a rocky path. Motioning me to mount behind him he drove slowly down a rough trail until we came to a road. Several kilometres on he turned into a clearing. A stone house stood between dark trees.

As we approached the house a small women emerged and spoke to the man who had brought me there. She was quite old, but moved briskly down a short passage and through a low door where four people were sleeping on mats. She placed her hand over her heart and gestured with open palms for me to lie on a mat alongside the others, bowed and back out of the room.

Early the next day they hid me in the back of a produce truck and drove me to the port where I boarded the passenger ship that was scheduled to leave for Haifa.

Rama

When the passenger ship docked in Haifa, I cleared through security using my false Swedish passport. During an earlier visit to the region I was initiated into a Druse family who lived in Rama, a hill town in *J'ebel Druse*. I decided to visit them rather than go at once to Sarai. Taking a bus to Acco I transferred to a sherut-taxi arriving late in the day at Rama. I had not walked five minutes up the twisting trail before they knew I was approaching.

Adib, my Druse blood-brother was descending to greet me. During an earlier visit I had been made a son of the family by declaration of his father, equal to his other children and a brother to Adib who was a teacher and minor official in the Arab school system. They were healthy Druse marked with the handsome features of their virile race, the color of their skin like the tint on fields at twilight.

Abu Hasib, Adib's father, was a good-looking man with kind eyes, a fine moustache, and a strong body. Hasib's intellect was perceptibly sharper than many villagers. He was a leader among the *Ugals* of the *Muwahhidin* (those of intelligence and highest order of rank in the Druse faith) and possessed a combination of abstract and active intellect. I sat late on the stone terrace with Adib and his father drinking tea. It was a night clear with the freshness of spring. Down in the village, tiny lamps wavered feebly like specks of ashes from a smouldering fire. Haifa's light was reflected on the night clouds to the west. To the east were lights from three towns on the Syrian plateau beyond Lake Galilee.

The following morning I woke early. Dawn flung its rays through the gnarled branches of olive trees in the orchards silvering their dark leaves. Abu Hasib's house perched on a clearing on the hill's slope overlooking a green valley embraced in an irregular grip by the uneven silhouette of the Galilee hills. Both the sea of Galilee and the Mediterranean could be seen from their terrace.

This was the heart of J'ebel Druse, rugged ranges rising from Syria through Israel to Lebanon, the stronghold of the Druse who settled here for safety after leaving Egypt eleven-hundred years after the Jews exodus.

The Druse are no nations servants. Honor is their highest premium. Their God, Jethro, is the father-in-law of Moses. Like the Jew's Messiah, Jethro is an immutable prophet, never directly addressed.

"Jethro may touch you," Abu Hasib said to me the night before. "You returned to us. Jethro knows why. You must know him like we do. The ways of your morals are not yet ours, but your eyes see us the way we are. No Druse will do you harm. My sons would die to save you. Should Adib harm you I would kill him." Abu Hasib said this with a disarming calmness, his confidence in Adib so strong, that I could not doubt him. Conversely my honor was being tested as well.

Before I left Rama, Adib took me by jeep to a Bedouin camp whose tribal Sheik was a life-long friend of his father. The sky overhead was porcelein blue. Wild orchids sprouted among buttercups and cyclamen, and poppies grew among green plants. The Bedawi were camped in a sparse forest south of the lake. The purpose of Adib's visit was not for me. It was agreed that I could wander down to the lake for an hour or so. However, at no time must I be left unprotected. Neither Syrian nor Israel patrols would treat me kindly if I strayed. Out of sight, two riflemen followed my path.

Perhaps an hour went by before I stopped near a marsh. I sat for a long while, my mind filtering years of detours and deceptions which led me to this point. Eight years away from my country and still I had not found the forms of life best suited for me. There was an emanation of loneliness about the site. A shadow passed above to darken the waves feebly licking the tired shore. It seemed that a night shade spread about me full of warning.

Murmuring to myself, pausing between thoughts I heard the croaking of frogs from the rushes, a bird's call, and gritty repetitious insect sounds in the marsh grass. Dry, inexorable cries in the mist drew me to some secret realm beyond myself. Over the skin of the lake a mist blew enveloping me with its chill. Afraid, I turned to the spectre beside me — a shadow with the head of a Caesar and the look of an eagle. While I watched, the face became that of a skull. In the feeble gloom the spectre whispered, "The eye of man and the beak of a vulture."

Jethro! Was this the sign of life, an omen of death? *Have you come to judge a life?*

The apparition slowly moved its skull from side to side, then raised its hand to point accusingly. Closing my eyes to block the image of its bony arm stretching towards me, I buried my head in my hands. Why my choice? Did he mean I must judge? Judge what? Judge whom? When I looked up and opened my eyes there was no one there. A yellow-brown pallor colored the ground beside me. There were no sounds, no cries in the marshes. A still death hung over the lake. I cannot say whether I remained stunned for minutes or an hour. Gradually the air stirred, rays of sunlight again shone on the rushes from which came the grating noises of insects. The Bedouin guards, who had waited in the distance came to guide me back to their camp.

The confrontation of that moment was a foreshadowing. The frightfulness of memory is like a dull blade pressing into my soul, more terrifying than anything save the certainty of death with pain. And the warning was painful, fierce and immeasurable.

When I went down to Nof Yam, I told Sarai about my disturbing experience. She did not discount my story or its portent. "You were touched by a very special spirit whose name you could not know."

"I believed that the apparition was Jethro. Is he a God, or prophet of the Druses?"

"We Semites see holy souls in many forms. In fact, the Druses do not directly address this priestly spirit who was the father-in-law of Moses. Jethro, or Jawa is another sounding, like Jesus, just as we Jews say Jehova which is a modern reconstruction of the ineffable Hebrew name of our Messiah, a god-guy whom we loaned to you Christians."

I watched Sarai while she talked. Her eyes were sad. On her face was an impression of a woman who understands frailty and who pities and forgives. A superb woman of her Sabra breed, Sarai had features that always excited me: a sensuous mouth, a handsome face and liquid eyes meeting mine. She smiled warmly when we embraced in greeting.

"Do you miss Avigdor?"

"Our sons miss him. Simon in particular. David has been waiting for you. We must buy a cake to surprise them after school. They are bigger than you can imagine. Of course you have to wrestle both of them together, and make them give up or you will lose face with them. They never stop telling what you can do, that their father cannot do"

"Has he written from Paris?"

"No, from New York. Nothing there for him. He hoped to do a sculpture in the Catskills, but they won't buy his dreams. His aunt in Brooklyn would not take him in. This is funny, he wrote that when he got to their place in the Bronx and started speaking Hebrew, they held their ears and told him to speak Yiddish. When he couldn't, they slammed the door in his face."

She shook her head in despair. "He writes that he cannot manage without me, that when he gets to Paris I must send him air fare to come home. It's a fortune to change Israeli lire to send money in French francs."

"I can give you dollars."

"Would you, as a loan?"

"Never mind. When he calls from Paris get an address and we'll send it to him. Will he sculpt again when he comes home?"

"I don't know? He has done nothing for a year, just plays with rocks by the sea."

"Do you want him back?"

"I want him whole again, that's all." Saying this she took my hand. "But you have not come to be burdened with my worries."

"Avigdor is my worry too."

"You are a true innocent, Mac. One of the few goys coming to our Promised Land with no fixed position about us. This is how Adib's father sees you. He senses your goodness. You are a Druse, a Jew, Christian and non-believer all in one. How did you come by this civility?"

"It was a gift proffered by women in my life. I don't dwell on faults in civilisation. Loving women like you nurtures my masculinity. I want women to use me as I use them. I am not always sure where I am going, but I know where I have been. I don't question the why of it. This is how I retain optimism. I keep searching and sharing my life. I don't give up."

"I have given up on Avigdor. I have nothing to offer him anymore. Avigdor is neither husband nor lover. When he is away I enjoy my freedom. But in another way I want him here. Everything is unreal whether he is home or not. Even you who I love as I loved Avigdor when he was like you, sweet and beautiful, could not keep me faithful. I know I should not be like this. I have become hard and arrid like cactus in the desert."

"Sarai you have years of reasons. You are a woman with great sensibility. Rational faculties wouldn't suit you.

Those are for prophets and rabbis."

"And you, with your trail of pregnant women crying when you leave them. Perfidy suits you. You look wonderful, thinner, but wonderful."

"Lovely liar," taking her hands in mine. If I looked half as wretched as I felt after that episode with Jawa, Sarai would have said much the same. I had in mind many things to confide, but they all jammed in my mouth when I kissed her.

Sarai raised her dark eyes to mine and said, with the purity of experience, "lay back, I know what you need."

A few days before Avigdor was due to fly home our intimacy was marred by her youngest son David coming home unexpectedly to get his football shoes for a school match. He was inside the bedroom before we realized, staring with disbelief, his mouth open to utter one word, "Mama," before turning to run out of the house.

David would not speak to us that evening at supper, and refused to go with his mother and brother to the airport the next morning to meet his father.

Alone with me David brought up what he saw in his mother's bed.

"I think I know what you and my mother were doing. I know she loves you. She doesn't love my father, so I think it's all right. Anyway, I am not going to tell my father."

"You are very grown up. Sarai and I will need your trust. More important, we must not hurt your father. He would understand that Sarai needs love, but not that his friend, and I am his friend, also loves your mother."

"Is my father very sick? Sometimes when I can't sleep I hear you talk about him."

"Your father is not sick in the way we think of someone being sick."

"How? You can tell me. I want to know how to be when he comes home."

"Your father is unsure of how to manage his life just now. Your mother and I are going to persuade him to sculpt again. He is confused and worried about you and your brother, the war and this country's future. Just be yourself with him. He needs your respect and love. Be his best friend."

"Are you our friend?"

"Yes and I always will be."

"You are my mother's friend, I know." Saying this, David went to the kitchen, returning with a pitcher of cold water and two glasses. "You won't make fun of me if I ask something about you and my mother, will you?"

"No, go ahead, ask me."

"Mother is different with you here. It must be what you were doing. Is it?"

"Partly, yes."

"Is it fun?"

"Well, yes. Something to feel good about with someone you like. Think how you feel when you walk home from school with that girl who lives up the street."

"But we don't do anything."

"Do you feel good inside when you are with her?"

"Yes. But I'll never do something to her. Not before we marry, if we do marry."

"Being with somebody special who also wants to be with you is the beginning of public love. What two people do in private is a stronger love.

"I suppose my mother has love with you. I know she wants you here." He smiled shyly, "Me too."

"Thank you, David. I am glad we talked about this. I feel like a second dad to you and Simon. Is that all right with you?"

"I would like you like a father if my mother would still be my mother."

This was getting heavy, and if it got back to Avigdor it would not be good. "What about us two keeping that idea a secret between us?"

"Can I tell my brother?"

"Maybe, but not right away. We'll see how things go when Avigdor is here. He might not like sharing you with me."

"Can we make blood the way Arabs do?"

"Make what?"

"Make me your blood son."

"All right, I would like that. Go get a razor blade." David rushed to find a blade. I nicked the skin of our wrists and held his slim arm over mine while our blood mixed. He stood before me beaming, kissed my cheek, wrapped his dirty kerchief around my cut, ran to get band-aids for us and skipped away a happy boy with a secret.

Yael

The week following my experience in that world of hallucination, for that is what I believed it was, I took a room near Dizengoff Street. I saw Avigdor in Café Kassit one night on that street. At first I hesitated about confronting him, but then thought, why not, He was thinner, but well. "Avigdor, welcome home, when did you get back?"

"A few days, why do you ask?"

"Curious, and from courtesy. Sarai is glad you returned safely no doubt."

"Yeah ... you stayed with her, then got a spell by the lake and fell in or something," Avigdor said with a grin.

"Or something like that. If that is what she said it's all right."

" Did you fly here direct from Paris?"

"You know I did. Sari said that you gave her money for my ticket. What did she do for it?"

I didn't like where his remarks were leading so I told Avigdor it was a loan.

"Where is Nelly? Why didn't she come? What did you do to her?"

"Nelly? You mean Nancy."

"Nelly, Nancy it sounds the same. Why didn't she come here with you?"

"She might have come, but we had a bad scene and now she's lost for me."

"You lose a lot of your women."

"What the hell, it happens."

"I liked her. She was good to me in Greece. You should have brought her." Slowly shaking his head, his lips tembling. Avigdor was clearly distressed about Nancy still back in Athens. "She told me she would come here, with or without you."

He tried to get more from me about our break-up, but I wasn't going to tell him. I did not let on that I was told about what happened between them in my Plaka retreat.

"Have you eaten yet? I'll treat you to dinner."

"No. You eat at my home tonight. Sarai is cooking something you like."

"Cooking what I like? I haven't spoken to her for days."

"I foretell events like a suitsayer."

"Soothsayer you mean."

"Yeah, that. I can find the enemy and you anywhere in Israel. Come on, I have an army jeep."

"Where did you get a jeep?"

"Borrowed it from an army depot."

We were like strangers riding to Nof Yam. I got hugs from their sons and a tongue kiss from Sarai when we entered their house warm with the flavor of my favorite couscous.

Simon and David were away at a youth event and we three had a fairly quiet dinner while consuming two liters of wine Avigdor had brought from France.

"We are what we have done with our time," I said.

"We must drink to what we have done, and who we are," Sarai offered, going to her cupboard for cognac and glasses. "Our life is an orgy of madness," Sarai said coming back to the table to pour the cognac. "We three are blessed with love's need of the flesh. This is what led you Avigdor, my husband, to go in search of truth essential to your nature," banging her glass against his glass with enough force to splash some cognac on his lap. Then turning to me, "you, Simon MacDonald, you move through affairs of the heart like the blood flows, nourishing women then going away as far away as you can, leaving babies for them to nurse."

"Ah, not quite like that, but not too far off the mark, Sarai. Still, my heart is not a stone. And there is no hole in my soul where my love for you two can escape.. I am moved by both of you and shall cherish evenings we have known like this."

Suddenly Avigdor laughed. I laughed with him. Sarai asked why we laughed. "Because in an odd way we need..."

"To laugh?"

"Each other."

"I need you more than you need me," Avigdor said.

Sarai agreed but her need was more physical than her husband's. Avigdor took his wife by the hand and trapped my waist with his arm, drawing us together, kissing his wife's cheek, then mine. We all laughed together, his laughter a little more hysterical than ours. I recited what Nancy said when I last saw her at the Ambassador's party. "Bitches and boys, and floys and goys, that is what family orgies are made of." Oh damn, I said family orgies. Freud would have a ball with that slip. Avigdor was spilling cognac onto the table trying to refill our glasses and I hoped he had missed what I said.

"It puts me to sleep in heat."

"I shouldn't," Sarai said, " Sleep robs you."

"You lack piquancy to arouse your husband drink!" He pulled Sarai onto his lap while gulping down his third cognac.

"Cousin," I said. "If each effort with your wife is a failure I can finish this bottle with you and bring myself to go down on both of you."

"Hah, you're crazy like Sarai. You need circum- circumstuffin, to mess with us Hebrews."

His trite response prevented me from doing anything or beating him before his wife.

"Would you like me to do both of you?" Sarai asked her husband.

"Why ask me? I don't think you care who does me."

"No, but we do," and taking Avigdor by the hand Sarai led him across the room, looking back toward me more than she should have. Avigdor grit his teeth, his face tortured with doubt and held onto his wife's hand. She went willingly with a shrug of her shoulders and a last look back to me, leaving me with the awareness of what she was going to have to do for her husband between the late hour and dawn.

Sarai made a beach picnic lunch for her family and me on my last Sunday with them at Nof Yam. We had about half a mile to walk to the beach in the warm spring sunshine.

175

Sodom and a Greek Passion

Nearing the sandy shore we saw a small brown dog running loose with its leash trailing. Some youngsters caught it to swing it round by its collar. A slim girl in a mauve bikini ran up to take the dog from them. While she was walking away more kids came around and began to tease her. David and Simon, who had gone ahead, ran down to chase them away. We watched while the girl went back to her belongings on the beach and secured her dog in the shade of a striped umbrella. She waved to the boys and ran into the water.

Sarai and I were poor swimmers. Avigdor and his sons were faster and went too deep for us. Sarai and I came out of the water to walk far up the beach hand in hand. While returning the boys ran up to say that Avigdor invited the girl to share our picnic. I could see she was not the child she appeared to be from afar. She was called Yael, age twenty-three, a tiny sexual being, a lithe bronze creature like a Yael, the Hebrew name for a Gazelle.

Yael had seen Sarai and me go off together and seemed surprised to learn that she was Avigdor's wife. I said that I was Avigdor's cousin and that Sarai was my favorite wife among my relations and that I loved her like her husband loved her.

Except for some common polite French phrases, I said little to the new girl. I watched while she spoke in Hebrew with Sarai and Avigdor. Sometimes Sarai would repeat her answers to me in English. I liked how Avigdor was with Yael. He was charming, interested and curious about her, like he had been when he met Nancy that morning in my Plaka room.. The boys jumped me so I wrestled them on the sand, pinning them both in a tangle amid yelps and exaggerated shouts of pain.

Yael's dog nipped me on the foot which ended our play.

She snatched it up to scold and smack it, but I took the dog from her and made it understand we were pals. I motioned that she should bandage the teeth marks her dog had made. She did so, using a napkin from her beach bag. Her slim fingers touching my ankle and foot aroused me. I did not try to hide my excitement, for I would have been unsuccessful.

Sarai laughed and said something to Yael in Hebrew. She looked into my face with a quick movement of her eyes, pulled the knot tight on my dog wound, smacked my leg and ran into the water after Avigdor and the boys.

"What did you say to her," I asked Sarai.

"I said you like her."

"That's all?"

"It was enough. She knew what I meant."

"Which was?"

"That you want her."

"You said more than you're telling me."

"I did. I told her you make love like a God."

"Sarai, you didn't?"

"I want you happy. Take her, Mac. She is clean and honest."

"How strange and beautiful she affects me. I do want her."

"Your hunger is obvious, and she recognized it. You'll have her."

"I'm afraid to frighten her, a new creature whom I know nothing about. What should I do?"

"I'll ask her to eat with us tonight. I'll play French songs on the piano after dinner. We'll finish off Avigdor's cognac and I'll take him to bed early. Then she's yours."

"It won't make you jealous?"

"No, no, you shared me, now I'll share you."

When Sarai asked Yael to dinner she first said she could not come. Then after persuasion, she thought she could get out of going to her sister's house where she was expected, but must first go home to call.

I took Yael to the path that led up the cliff towards Nof Yam. When she stepped up on a rock I kissed each cheek and shook her hand the way French do. Then I watched her and the dog walk off around the curve in the path.

By half past eight Yael had not come. David and Simon were fed and made ready for bed. Avigdor thought Yael would not show up. Sarai was sure she would. Simon did not care, but David did. He was pleased when Yael appeared at the open door, her dog rushing in ahead of her.

I watched her at dinner, dark unspoiled face with high cheeks, smiling with small even teeth and questioning eyes ranging over us. She wore the Seal of Solomon on a gold chain around her bronze neck. Pleasure, I thought, would be taken gladly with this girl.

It was like that later, sweat on her upper lip licked by her quick tongue, black strands of hair pasted to her neck and temples, smiling up at me with her deep eyes watching my features joyful in pleasure.

She drank a small glass of wine during the meal, nothing stronger after the dinner while we listened to Sarai play piano. Avigdor was hesitant about drinking too much that night. Sarai and I looked at each other from time to time, watching Yael and Avigdor with amusement. The conspired seduction could not come off. I knew anyway that I would not ask her to bed in their house.

Before midnight I took her to the bus stop. But the last one had already left. It was several miles to her parent's house in Herzylia. We went slowly through sparse woods beside an army barracks where a sentry challenged us when her dog barked. Yael spoke in Hebrew and he let us pass. Before the woods ended near her settlement we lay down on the soft dirt under a cool sky spotted with stars.

Nearing her house we stopped and kissed. "Will you be with them tomorrow night?"

"Yes."

"Wait for me by the woods at twilight where you made love to me."

We lost the dog's leash. I said I would search our path in the morning and find it. But I did not go back to Nof Yam that night. I lay down on the earth that had marked our bodies and slept until dawn.

Fate was somehow entangled with my coming on to Yael. Within the month she was to enter her second year in residence at the teacher's training institute in Beersheba. We were to be in that city together more than a year. Involvement with her had a lot to do with tilting the complex of my injudicious life as witnessed in Greece, into something quieter, reflective, and bearable.

Yael's love stemmed from fundamental hunger — mine from satiety. Over the next year it developed into a deeply felt drama of growth for both of us.

The Negev

My second interview with the engineering firm arranged my work terms and salary, subject to security clearance by Israel. I must move to Beersheba for an interview and to await the outcome before becoming an accessory to Spoon River Corporation's Sodom fabrication.

The separation of ties with Nof Yam and the impact of Yael tilted my spirit towards an unbalanced misanthropy. When not on the job I stayed in my room. It wore on me. I had no desire to visit Beersheba's bars or brothels. When I crossed the point of darkness between Greece and Israel I was prepared to share Sarai's love, but not have another. Still that seemed a good chance for my soul and body to be soothed by a woman less troubled than Sarai. But it was too soon. I was not able to support an added burden on my heart so recently rent by Nancy.

Why had I gone so far away? Not to continue habits from that Grecian world of confusion, but that is what I did. There in that sandy market post on the fringe of history I penetrated the eroded desert strewn with broken faiths, exploring sunken and melancholy places under relentless skies, the whole scene a lyrical comment on the aridity of existence.

I quickly became lost with no sense of direction. Dizzied by day with torrid wind and sun, chilled by night with dew, I was shamed into pettiness by the changing heavens. In the gloom of the desert an attraction of ghostly confusion spread before me, a spiritual beckoning of faith that I could not comprehend affected my reason.

In the morning it was hot, but dry. By noon the heat was unbearable. After eating some figs I tried to continue but lacked the force. I dug into the baked ground near a crumbling rock mound and lay in a narrow hollow to sleep. When I awoke it was night. I moved on towards a far off splash of light that I thought might be Bae'r Yeroham. But could not continue and sunk down again.

While the night wore on I slept fitfully. Every sense alerted me to rise and go on. It differed from other nights because of warm winds descending, stirring nothing around then vanishing leaving no freshness. A *khamsin* threatened. This forced me to get up and go on just before dawn. I never knew when the sun rose. The sand, hot and baleful, crowded me like a smothering caress. A frightening silence wove itself in the stifling sheet covering the desert. Hung in the midst of the terror, an exaggerated red reflection mocked. Length after length of thick murk blocked the sky, smothering the hills and valleys with thick heat. No insects or birds were there. The *khamsin* imprisoned me and everything else on the land.

Before twilight the sandstorm was spent. A military squad in a halftrack saw me at once. Soldiers took me up, washed my lips with water, and tried to get response from me in Arabic and Hebrew. Their insignia was of the Druse battalion stationed at Bae'r Yeroham. I pronounced the family name of Adib, my Druse brother from Rama. They knew his father Abu Hasib. From a suspected person I was treated as an unusual find — a stranger speaking neither Hebrew nor Arabic who was familiar with their villages in the north.

The following week I returned to Nof Yam to await acceptance by the Spoon River Engineering firm. The threat of what could have happened to me in the Negev made Avigdor and Sarai afraid for me. They said to forget the Sodom work and stay by the sea with them.

"Forget about that job in Sodom. The land surrounding Beersheba is dangerous, and the road to the Dead Sea is too great a risk for you. We need you here."

"Thanks Sarai, but I believe it is time for me to leave. Avigdor needs you without me in the way."

Avigdor wanted to know about the beach girl. "Have you seen her often? Are you making out with her?"

"No," I lied. I did not want Sarai to hear about the mating on the soft earth our first night together after Yael's visit to their home. "She plans to enroll in a teaching seminary near Beersheba next month. I expect to take up with her then."

Sarai was a clever woman and better, a dear woman. She sent Simon to Yael's home with a message for her to come that night.

When Yael arrived with Simon there was a puzzling appeal on her face. Partly it was alarm about what Simon had told her about my ordeal in the desert. Before saying anything to me she did something that amused David and Simon, which surprised Avigdor and delighted Sarai. She kissed and hugged each of them in turn.

Sarai came beside me, whispering, "Treasure her, she is good for you."

Yael pointed her finger at me, scolding, "I was trained in the Negev, you go only with me after now."

Well, I was in no position to object knowing that Sarai was anxious for me to have Yael, a woman who would care for me like she had done.

From the time we met on the beach, and even after our intimacy I had not yet been concerned beyond the physical because I did not think about a future with Yael. During the days before leaving Nof Yam, I began to admire her fine features, her golden flesh, hazel eyes, patrician nose and wide lips ready for wickedness. I came to know every line and pose of that young woman with her youthful silhouette both fragile and athletic.

Yael was sensuous, reckless in passion, always craving, always ready to be taken. I reveled in her challenge when she dashed up the beach like a boy daring me to catch her. We sunbathed in isolation on a favorite ledge among beach cliffs forged by erosion. My heart explored her heart, my lips devoured her bronze flesh shaping her breast, hips and thighs. My masculine homeliness paired with her beauty, experience meshed with her feminine grace, wooed us to fuck in the shuddering heat. I lifted her to lay over me so that I could look at her dark eyes beaming soft pity on me with an eloquence I had never before seen in a woman's eyes.

Finished, hands clasped over her black hair, Yael sang snatches of poetry over the blinding slivers of waves dancing towards France and the Europe I wanted to tell her about. Born in

Jerusalem

Jerusalem, jewel in a wracked area. To dwell here Aarabs, Jews, Romans, Byzantines, Druse, Turks, Palestians, British and the new Israelis have all been singed in its searing climate. This spiritually tortured city has suffered and survived them all.

A tangled hybrid, tough, sinful and human, Jerusalem's spiritual quality has guided the numen of its bloody history until now when a new and precarious civilization has spread over what is old, fatigued and damaged.

Deathless spirits from the restless past pervade the sun-blessed hills to stir the universal love for the separated brethren divided by vengeful prophets astride the porous wailing wall.

What a deceptive scene viewed from Jehovah's privy. Every dirt path, every stone house and dry wadi is prickly with emotive charge and cursed suffering. Old Jerusalem was denied to the Jews since the Ninth legion of Emperor Titus destroyed it and scattered the tribes throughout a hostile world seventy years before Christ. Thirteen hundred years the Jews wandered in the Diaspora weighing themselves on the scales of Western civilization, measuring if the goyim were hanging in with.

What had they endured through the last crucible before coming to Zion? No pogrom in history has equaled the holocaust designed by twentieth century Christian killers inhabiting the new Europe.

But the early crusading mauraders set the example, displaying their piety by slaying Muslims in their mosques and burning Jews in the synagogues, then when the Jew's prophet was crucified split *His* teachings into a divinity of death.

Eternal Love

Several days before I was to go live in Beersheba, Sarai and I had our last affair in their Nof Yam home. We did not need to talk out the nature of our love that we knew would be forever. We simply got at each other, fearing that it might be the last time we would lie together naked.

Our need for one another was deeper than I could see. Sarai was better equipped to judge life and the human forces that distort love. Who knows better the variants of the human mind than a woman who has accompanied her husband to the brink? And she did feel the waste of him posing, strutting, shedding his colorful thoughts like a hard flower on the desert's crust, whose roots a foot down wither in the hot earth.

Avigdor came from his bedroom murmuring, "What's to care? Only a fool in love gives a damn for what will be." Walking nude past us, he smiled, snatched his cognac bottle from the table and poured some on our bodies before going back to his room.

There was no moral mystery to unravel here. I had long ago adjusted to the wry devices of love. The common primal crime of adultery is no more sinful than a second digestive. Love, after all, is an imaginative expression designed by man's genius and viewed by each woman in her own way.

Avigdor had an uncle who owned a small hotel at the edge of Mia Sharim, the ultra-orthodox quarter in Jerusalem where Hebrew is the language of prayer, and Yiddish is the people's street language. Had the *Yeshivim* become aware that a Jewish maiden and an American goy were pleasuring in sin next to their quarter they would have burned the hotel, and stoned us.

Avigdor was given a permanent room there in exchange for occasional work for his uncle at the hotel. He gave me a key and said that I could use the room anytime on condition that Sarai must never know, and I should not use that room with anyone but Yael.

Yael and I shared a great deal there on quiet holy weekends. We loved and respected one another in a way I had forgotten was possible. We had only English in common. My French was inadequate to express myself poetically, my Hebrew was worse. Not able to know much about each other kept our companionship and love easy. There was a compulsion to do something about it, to fill in the silence. Impulses were released through animal channels without reliance on wordy artifice. It was far better that way for I would have told things I was not ready to tell, and Yael was not ready to receive.

Each time we were alone in that hotel room, an eerie sense of familiarity with the place disturbed me. When I realized why I could not explain it to her — in fact I dared not.

I arrived late one Shabbath morning and found kneeling before a bookcase. Then I knew what was bugging me about the place. Except that the books were in Hebrew, instead of English, this place was weirdly similar to Don Lucas' room in Athens when Nancy and I had an unforgettable love-in there. Then the Greek world with my friends, Donald, Avigdor and Nancy was spiritually linked to me that happy Greek morning on Syntagma square.

My god! Yael was even wearing a Bedouin dress that she found in the closet, not unlike the robe Nancy wore in Lucas' room in Plaka. Nancy remarked on the place and asked things about Avigdor that Nancy had asked about Lucas.

"Do you think Avi reads all these books? He has so few at his home with Sarai?"

"Don't know. They may belong to his uncle."

"What does Avigdor do now?"

"Nothing. Avigdor was a fine sculptor. Now he does nothing. Sarai lets him play with his stones in their garden. She keeps him fed and in drink."

"I don't see any pictures of Sarai here, and none of their sons either."

I really could not listen to her questions, nor produce any more answers about Avigdor. She sensed that I was up tight and mistook it for my need to fuck her.

"Never mind him," she said, "let me get at that curved sculpture of yours."

I wasn't surprised that Yael was nude under that Bedouin dress, like Nancy was in Athens. How eerily matching was Yael's passion this Shabbath morning with Nancy's ardor that Greek morning. Her fervor lifted me into a dual space between Athens and Jerusalem with two lovers performing the same acts. Four hands were clawing my flesh, two mouths tasting me. Holy Moses, they were twin clones of Lilith, that demonic worm-holed strumpet with serpents oozing from their wombs to strangle my penis. I never again returned with Yael to that hotel room alongside Mia Sharim.

Ein Karim

In midsummer Sara and Avigdor moved from Nof Yam to live in a damaged Arab house in Ein Karim that was taken by the government after Jerusalem wrest half the city from Jordan. The ancient village lies among dark cypress and silvery olive trees above Wadi Hanina that separates Ein Karim from Jerusalem. The second story balcony of their house looked on the Italian Church of the Visitation, marking the place where Mary fled while pregnant with Jesus to hide from her family and husband Joseph who was troubled about her condition.

Avigdor had teamed with Guilat Rosen, a local sculptor, to execute a series of murals on the garden walls of the church. One point in the church court is believed to be the site where John the Baptist was born.

Three years earlier Guilat and Avigdor directed a team of artists and stone masons to assemble a mammoth project with huge slabs of black stone cut from Solomon's Mines to be erected at the atomic research center near Ashkalon, west of Tel Aviv. They were the idols of the cultural elite that year.

Guilat was supposed to meet the three of us in Jerusalem to mark the third anniversary of their award-winning ceremony. We waited at an illegal underground club that served drinks during Friday Shabbath nights and Saturday until dawn, but Guilat did not come.

About sunup we three walked up to King David's tomb on Mount Zion. The tomb was close to the Church of the Holy Sepulcher located in the Old Christian quarter. In Arabic this sacred city is El Kuda, in Hebrew Yerushalayim. On the mount we were watching a golden inflammation over eastern hills rising to light the earth's rim. The sun rose with huge pleasure to warm the dome and the noble wall of ocher-colored stones that formed a wall of Herod's temple built by Sulemain the Magnificent.

Descending slowly, Sarai and I watched her husband walking ahead of us shaking his head, lifting both arms to embrace all Palestine. He stopped and turned towards us, tears clouding his light eyes, "How they have used and turned us to fear our cousins."

"Who does he mean?" I asked Sarai.

"The Zionists. Avigdor doesn't like them. We New Jews are all the victims of their persuasions."

"Are you not the recipients of their cunning too?"

Avigdor looked at me with sadness. "There is more life in Hebrew myths than living them."

I said to them, "Some years ago in New York I saw a play called *'Moses'* by Rosenberg. I did not understand how he meant the audience to take these lines:

Yesterday as I lay nigh death with toil
underneath the hurtling crane oiled with our blood,

Thinking to end all and let the crane crush me,
He came by and bore me into the shade.
O what a furnace roaring in his blood
Thawed my congealed sinews and tingled my own
Blood raging through me like a strong cordial.
He spoke, since yesterday
The streaming vigours of his blood erupting
From his halt tongue is like an anger thrust
Out of a madman's piteous craving for a monstrous
baulked perfection.

We were quiet after I recited the verse that I had read and reread, crossing the Atlantic on the Queen Elizabeth eight years before. They have never left my memory since. "Is this propaganda or poetry?"

"We Jews use all media to convince gentiles of our worth," Sarai remarked with a hint of irony.

"I was raised by poetry," Avigdor said, still in tears. "When I was a boy my father would take me to the desert to watch streams of myths flow past. He could recite whole passages of the Book of Gensis by heart. He was born in a British-run hospital in the same ward where Arab mothers gave birth.

"My mother told me that when she was a student she passed my father's house and there was always a light in his room. She said that, one night he caught her looking in his window He invited her her to climb in. And she did. When they married she set one room aside for him alone to study and write."

"My father and his brothers tilled the land with Arab fathers and brothers who shared the crop and trusted each other. When the Palestinians were driven away in forty-eight my father cried and left the land for good. He died holding a book."

Sarai said that her grandfather was a telling influence for her and her sister. "He would take us to the kibbutz he helped create in 1903 after he fled Russia with his young wife. In the kibbutz meeting hall, used on Shabbath for a synagogue, and for a library during the week. There were hand-written notebooks bound with ribbon stored beside aging sacred scrolls in the libraty archives. He would carefully unwrap the pages and translate the Russian, Polish and Yiddish script written by Ashkenazi survivors seeking refuge in this promised land. They were not tales of Goliath fantasy or accounts about clearing land and splashing through reed bogs to drain malaria pockets in Galilee swamps. The comments were texts of anguish, complaints, vengeance and curses written by despairing refugees, the same kind of security-haunted Jews who immigrate here today. In the process the children of intellect were siring peasants to waste in battle with our Semitic cousins. I sometime wonder whether the Zionist political aim intended that we endure consistent chaos and war in order to prevent us Jews from sharing this wondrous historic land with Allah's chosen."

While Sarai talked, Avigdor was seated on the pavement. There were tears in his eyes looking up to me and his wife..

"After we were married I took Avigdor to the kibbutz to read those chronicles. We bribed the librarian, who was the Rabbi, to let us read and copy from them. The Rabbi was an old man who knew my grandfather. A lot of the pages were damaged or missing. We smuggled out half of the journals to photocopy and translate. We found an editor who published them. The kibbutz council sued. The editions were placed under bond to the court nearly ten years ago. I am sure we will never see them again in public. Only two mythologies are crammed into Israeli young; the ancient unproven, and the promise of a dream state unsullied by non-Jews."

"Perfidy!" Avigdor shouted from the pavement.

This whole scene with them was bizarre. I did not know how to react to what they were saying. Until then I had not heard Israelis criticize their rabbis and government with such emotion. I recited that promise in the scripture: "And they shall come that were lost in the land of Assyria, and they that were dispersed in the land of Egypt."

Sarai was now kneeling on the paving comforting her husband. Rising slowly she pulled Avigdor to his feet. "Enough of this, I know a café where we can have breakfast."

Left unsaid that morning was the anxiety they felt for Simon and David. They did not want their sons to choose early, like their father had to choose, to be familiar with destiny, and fear premature death. I tried to understand and feel like a Jew, but did not succeed. I had no sons in Israel, nor was I marked with the burden of their potent faith.

Staggering from fatigue when we got to Ein Karim I lay down fully clothed. I vaguely heard Sarai begging Avigdor not to drink, then nothing while I slept the whole day through. It was dusk when I was wakened by Sarai kissing me. She had to stop when the tea kettle whistled. I looked in on Avigdor who was snoring softly. I sat on the edge of his bed to put on slippers. Sarai brought a tray with small copper cups around the steaming

Sodom and a Greek Passion

tea kettle. I shook Avigdor to wake him. His mouth moved to a smile, then he opened his eyes and asked if Sarai and I had played with each other while he was sleeping.

Well, we had been doing just that. We were unable, in fact, unwilling to discipline our sexual avarice. The psychic plot of that evil became art. Sarai decided that this art should conjure beauty from the banal practice of adultery, that the reverse of morality was love's truth. Of course I was a *shmuck* to sleep under Avigdor's roof and lay with his wife. And I was consciously unfaithful to Yael also.

The next weekend, Yael and her entire class of teaching students were sent to a military training kibbutz near the Golan Heights bordering Syria to conduct classes with young soldier recruits.

My Shabbath weekends, by invitation from Sarai, were in Ein Karim. Avigdor's behavior that summer was decidedly errant, the most bizarre I had ever witnessed by a man who could be wonderfully amusing and completely wacky within the space of an hour. Sarai and I were culpable contributors to his madness. We had to share excesses of alcohol with Avigdor until he passed out so that we could get at each other. It was a deceit Sarai and I contrived to shift our anguish to Avigdor. All the salt in the Dead Sea could not smart her husband's wounds more than how we chafed him with our behavior.

When I was there to comfort Sarai, she could tolerate her husband's behavior, his mocking of orthordox values, his anxiety about their sons, his suspicions, accusing her of every form of depravity — depravity which indeed Sarai and I shared. On some nights he declared himself the

Messiah. When agitated, Avigdor's energy and spirit appeared younger as though discontent, war, frustration and drink heightened his spirits, while time stood still like it cannot for Christians and other *Goyim*.

He displayed at other times the sly cunning of the possessed stirred in with his nonsense. "Jawah offers this *merde* through me; the soul of infidels, the soul that is subject to a devil's freedom will perish, but Jewish souls, ah, Jewish souls alone will survive, and maybe — maybe even your soul," pointing to me, "an honorary Jewish soul by injection."

It was in this damaged house where I feared that Sari's troubled husband might hurt one of us. To enter the vaulted bedroom and salon on the second floor of their damaged house a wooden ladder was tied to the terrace rail. The door from the terrace had a rusty latch that scraped when turned.

One afternoon Sarai was nude playing Brahms at her piano. I had just left the shower room and was toweling my wet body when I faintly heard the ladder to the balcony scrape. Motioning for Sarai to go to her bedroom, I hastily got into Avigdor's robe, picked up a book and sat down by the window pretending to read.

I want to describe exactly how Avigdor behaved when he saw me. His body had the stiffness of an animal, his head moving back and forth trying to scent what was wrong in his domain. Mouth set in a grim line he took in the scene, the open bedroom, my obvious nakedness beneath his robe. Taking down an ornate scabbard from the wall he slowly drew the curved blade, walked towards me and used the tip if the knife to turn the book over to see the title, grunted, then awkwardly turned to go toward his bedroom. He looked back at me grinning, and stepped inside.

I hesitated to move after him for fear it would arouse him to use the dagger on one of us. Because there was no cry from Sarai I stayed put. Soon he backed out of the room laughing, then turned to face me. In place of the dagger his hand was closed over a hard erection.

Nearly Wed

My work in Sodom was nearing its end. The installation was completed, replacement material and spare parts ready to hand over to the Dead Sea Works and there was not much to keep me there.

With the end of an eposide in sight fugutive memories began to return to my sleep. They illuninated nothing, explained nothing, but I thought that I saw them as some kind of warning. Did I want to go off alone once more?

My life paused, the future seemed like a graveyard without hope. It suddenly came to me that I wanted to marry Yael. The idea shook me, Under the shower I felt clean. Doubts were shed with my soiled clothing. The discarded garments were not all I shed. The web of my careless past began to unravel, falling from my shoulders like a shroud of dishonor. My carnal selfishness had caused me to faulter at every stage untill now. It was time to end that injudicious play.

Jewish women in Israel and the men they want to marry must prove that they are Jews. Marriage is not possible otherwise.

That was our obstacle. Because of Yael's parents the marriage would have to be an orthodox ceremony. Yael and I determined to bring it about with help from Sarai and Avigdor. Rabbinical courts in some towns are lenient when accepting testimony by two witnesses. Doubt was involved in some suggestions, and then a plan agreed on, which was dropped because of its risk, and because of a better idea suggested by Avigdor.

I was to present myself at a selected court using my Beersheba address. Avigdor would testify that I was his cousin, a plausible fib since we both had light eyes. My mother's birthplace was to be Odessa, the port city on the Black Sea. her name Luba Gudinov, the same as Avigdor's grandmother. In truth she was Laura MacDonald born in St. Louis, Missouri. Yael's best friend would have her husband speak for me. Should the three Rabbis accept my witnesses, I would get a certificate declaring me a bachelor and a Jew. Then Yael and I could marry.

Avigdor was entrusted to the task of arranging the deception. In the meantime I dealt with Yael's father over the dowry, was out-bargained and paid in advance three times more than was customary in *Sphardi* marriage deals.

Her portly father, who called himself Rabbi Solomon, was a former colonial post master in Algeria, who spoke in vernacular French and prayer Hebrew. He had little formal schooling and was an uncouth spiritualist who feared dying without a prayer in his lips. He prayed two hours at dawn, at table during meals, and part of each hour of the twenty-four between Friday twilight and Saturday dusk. Solomon's Rabbi title was dubious, acquired when he took over a small synagogue in Algeria outside Constantine when the true Rabbi fled during the Franco-Algerian war. Solomon conducted extreme orthodox sessions with the Jews who remained until the last days of the rebellion when they either fled to France, or immigrated to Israel. He did not seek a synagogue posting in Israel, so his title was not questioned.

Madame Solomon, a quiet, obedient, kind woman, born a Muslim, married Solomon when she was fifteen. A certificate issued by Rabbi Solomon's bogus office attested to an orthodox marriage with him. Yael made me promise not to tell anyone about her father's rabbinical trick.

Rabbi Solomon, trapped by a history he did not comprehend, displayed a monumental ignorance about the world beyond Algeria. Like a great many Jews who emigrated from Arab nations in North Africa he was as unaware of the machinations of the Zionist party to bring about the State of Israel as he was about what went on in Europe under the Nazis.

Seldom in his life had Papa Solomon read a lay book or read literature not filled with praise of Judaism and the Torah. Any questions put to him about religion were replied to in that slightly bemused tone used when one repeats what has long been known and decided. He really did not know how unbelievably cruel Europe was to the Jews.

Avigdor was les than sober when he entered the Rabbinical court the day of my hearing. Smiling to the three bearded Rabbis, Avigdor mumbled the bogus evidence we had rehearsed, "...mother of applicant a refugee from Odessa, his father a Dutch Jew...both passed on to Paradise." Then, as an afterthought, Avigdor remembered that we were cousins. Giggling throughout his presentation, his skull cap slipping from his head, Avigdor went skipping out of the court when they asked for the second witness. There was no second witness because Avigdor forgot to tell him to come that day. That ended our plot to present myself a Jew for the purpose of marriage.

Beersheba

Life seems less menacing when there is a woman to embrace. After a long day working down on the Dead Sea. Yael was my comfort in Beersheba. When she could not be with me for supper I would go to rest in her room at the teaching institute while she and her roommate studied. The twelve hours expended to journey down to Sodom, contribute a day's work and return to Beersheba, were physically and mentally tiring.

When I arrived back from working in Sodom I showered, drank something cool and about nine o'clock crawled into bed. Some mornings I awakened to find Yael there. She had come late, quietly undressed and lay down with me. Other times she was waiting in my room when I came up from the Dead Sea, her perfumed flesh coming to me, soothing and caressing my heat-sore body. She was so earthly human, so wholly dedicated to making me happy. Her *Spharidim* savagery, her French sophistication at love filled my soul indescribably.

I liked the work challenge, but before my first year work year was up I was longing to escape those technicians who could never be my friends.

They were no testimonal for the morale of the people back in America who recognize civil rights as a term with meaning. Just as they fail to understand the ethos of Negroes in their home land, they made no effort uo understand the struggle of Jews and Palestinians in their sacred land.

The descent to the Dead Sea in spring is beautifully shaped and colored. In summer the climatic conditions in Sodom are as racking as can be conceived. During winter's rain the desert blooms with ragged clumps of stunted bushes and wild flowers in damp gullies, Irides, poppies, red anemones and cyclamen nourish from the dew before the hot sun forces their colorful heads to bow.

The construction at the Dead Sea was a wet-process potash plant that cost an estimated twenty million dollars. Its site
was two miles away from an older plant that had been processing the rich mineral silt from the Dead Sea for half a century. Between the two sites was a bromide plant fuming noxious gold clouds over the construction site.

The gathering of material was a tremendous exercise: steel from Italy, generators from France, glass-lined tanks from Britain, electric devices from Switzerland, forged piping from Germany, tooled machines from Scandinavia, and thousands of tons of material from nearly every State in America. The work was under way when I joined the Spoon River Construction project. All of this was going on within the range of a long mortar shot from the hills of Jordan beyond the lake.

A caste system prevailed at the work site: thirty-five Americans were top dogs, Israeli engineers from the Dead Sea

Works were next in line. Local contractors and hired specialists like myself were middle level, followed by Israeli laborers. Lowest on the economic rung were Druse work teams contracted through a sheik from their villages in the north. They labored for thirty-day periods in the hell-heat of Sodom before they had a week off to visit their families. Native Arabs, whether Christians or Muslims were not hired on sites along any Arab borders.

Spoon River's Americans behaved like colonialists, their superior on-site behavior an egocentricity communicable more by the source of their salary than overt bossism. They were experienced specialists dedicated to technical know-how, taking pride in intelligent use of top quality material. There was never a doubt that they would successfully create a viable operating process for the inexhaustible supply of rich potash lying in the Dead Sea.

What astounded me was how they were so prolific in practical matters and even in most forms of basic logic, yet remained unconscious of their own biased absurdities.

History has never seen such a great nation parade its wealth, guns and arrogance for the cause of manifest destiny. The face of a rebellious sentiment within America's Black population was, to them, an anomaly. The aspirations of displaced Palestinians were beyond their understanding.

My lone dissenter's voice trying to shake their conceit was inadequate and hilarious. Unless a sentence expressed a compliment embellishing free enterprise, sacred capitalism, religion, justice, and Godly morality, its dissenting structure wounded their ears. Those pedestrian Protestants were dedicated to the proposition that democracy really exists. They

Sodom and a Greek Passion

could not get into their insular minds that different political circumstances create different desires in people. In the morning heat it was already too hot to touch the car metal by six-thirty. Riding past the old plant, the grating, groaning machinery pounded away like the regional rhythms of ethnic hate and self-deception.

The work conditions would have been unbearable if I did not have a woman like Yael.

One weekend we went to the Negev Desert on the Eilat bus, leaving it at Sede boqer, the kibbutz retreat of Ben Gurion. Behind the kibbutz, dusty tracks lead to Wadi Magdol, a rugged earth fualth with perhaps the loveliest colouring in the Negev. Raw and riven gorges radiated the sun in myriad shimmering reflections of color. Hues changed like a kaleidascope with the time of day.

We stood side by side in the hot sun on the edge of the rift into whose depths no breeze ranged to relieve the slow saturation of heated air. About a mile or so down the wadi a slow line of camels bearing huge bundles were heading slowly in the direction of Jordon.

We descended part way down the Wadi slope to shade behind overhanging rocks. We ate and drank sparingly in the dry heat, pressed our hot bodies together, then slept. Twilight was on us when we woke. A slow spread of useless beauty moved down theWadi until night shade erased their tones. The low sun gave way in the haze to a quarter moon and countless stars.

Yael was like a painting against the star-pure sky, a breathless profile of woman, her dark head moving with the rhythm of her voice. I had taught her some gospel songs that

Nancy had sung to me. Yael sung what verses she could remember of "Jacob's Ladder" and "Sometimes I Feel Like A Motherless Child".

I closed my eyes and believed that Nancy was singing to me, not Yael. They were tearing when she finished.

"Love always and take care of me," Yael said, breaking my reverie. "Why?" she asked, "why do you like me, or love me?"

"By sharing what I feel about you, Yael, I am sustained during the long hours we are apart. It makes me trust you. And trust is what I feel from you."

She looked at me, apprehension and doubt showed on her dark features, her lips trembling, searching the meaning of what I was saying. "Only trust? Not love?"

"Well, we are in love no doubt, but to declare only that I love you, and believe that you truly love me, is a sentiment we have not reached yet. That is the next stage we are climbing to, and honestly I am not sure if we have touched the summit yet."

I suppose I was not explaining myself very well. Yael turned away slowly shaking her head, then began to cry.

The silence that intruded on us following my clumsy attempt to define our relationship was uncomfortable. She did let me hold her, until tears stopped flowing, finally saying softly to Nancy had sung to me. Yael sung what verses she could remember of "Jacob's Ladder" and " Sometimes I Feel Like A Motherless Child".

me, "*C'est bonne,* it's good you guard some of your love away from me. I understand. And I will never forget how we were before now. I am too soon for you after your girl in Greece.

You can still want her, I don't mind. You love Sarai, and that is all right too. And I know that you will always want me, like I want you. Whatever you do to me here I will always desire your body. And when we are apart, I will always feel your caresses. And when you leave me, like men like you always leave women who love you, our souls will touch wherever we be in the world. And never, never will I forget you before I die--never."

I was to remember later all that she said then, when it tore into my heart, quivering there like a thrown knife. I said nothing because of the shadow that lay between us.

Why on earth did I cling to Sarai, and the memory of Nancy? Yael was somebody wholly mine. Perhaps they were extensions of each other. One love was simpler, formed through empathy.. The other rooted in passion. Where would Sarai's husband fit when all was unraveled? In a way the four of us were of the same mind, each taking something from the other, taking more than anyone could give back. Confusion informs us less how to love than where to find it. Was this the edge of a new departure, or a repetition of earlier disappointments?

Bedouins

Adib was expected in Beersheba about a week before my Sodom work would end. Earlier on we had spoken about something of interest to me that could not be discussed openly. Unwittingly I included Avigdor without thinking of a complication. The morning I awaited Adib, Avigdor came to Beersheba while I was selecting my belongings for moving the next week. He was sober and had not a hint of contrition, and no apology for fucking up my wedding.

"Adib here yet?"

I replied that he was on his way.

Avigdor put a flame under my coffee pot, watched the coffee stir to a boil, then said without turning: "You may be angry with me, or you may not. A hammer stroke from a cloud rattled my brain the night before the judgment. I was afraid for you. Sarai had heard something about a trap to get you for claiming to be Jewish. Sarai was afraid they might suspect you are a spy. I was not going to be there, but I drank that day for courage to go there.

I reached for some coffee and waved off his apology.

"It's okay, I wasn't angry — just annoyed. Yael and I will work something out. Maybe we'll go to Cyprus where Goy guys and born-again Jewish virgins can marry."

"Yael." He spoke her name as though it was unfamiliar to him.

"My life this week has been hell because of my fiasco."

"Sarai giving you hell?"

"Madame has more need for you than I care to note."

Adib's jeep stopped in front. He came in eager for the adventure arranged for us.

The road out of Beersheba branches south at *B'aer Yeroham* to traverse the Negev desert down to the Gulf of Aqaba. It replaces the old road that runs close to the Jordan frontier. Its branches lead to archaic sites, past grazing camels and Bedouin encampments to Israel's atomic plant beyond Dimona. The Negev's most unique feature is Wadi Raman, fearsome and desolate, like some flaw punched in the earth at the time of creation. It straddles the width of the scarred and wrinkled upland in the central desert region. The road twists down three thousand feet to its valley floor. The cruelly parched valley is scarred by earth faults which, during winter rains carry streams of brown water. Its rocky citadels have always been a haven for the spiritually hungry.

Somewhere in Wadi Raman was the encampment Adib was seeking. After an hour's rough drive Adib turned the jeep off the road to go up a dry tributary towards the west into strange hills deserted but for a few ragged tents perching on the slopes of desolation. Nearing noon the sun was high, its brilliance obliterating any distinctiveness of shape and substance, tinting everything in a film of sameness. We passed straggling groups of sheep and goats tended by tiny creatures like scarecrows, probably young girls muffled in dark garments.

In the blinding light I did not see the opening into a gully until we turned to drive through where a rifleman was seated on a rock. A sheik and his guards were waiting quietly in front of a goatskin tent when Adib left the jeep to approach them. He embraced an elderly thin man who wore a green scarf which marked him as the sheik. He beckoned for us to approach and led us inside.

I was the object of much curiosity. Adib's information that I was his blood brother from far away was doubtless the cause. The Sheik's son asked Adib if I was a Jew.

I shook my head.

The Sheik said something to Adib who translated.

"He believes you are religious because of your beard."

Again I shook my head.

"Do you have another belief from your people, he now asks?"

"The universe, the spirit of the soul," I said for Adib to translate. How could I tell these believers that I am agnostic?

Except for his eldest son, Mohammed Ali, no one had any knowledge about a city called Chicago, or where it was in America. Few of them had even heard of Paris or Athens. Few had been as far north as Haifa since Israel was reborn. They spoke through Ali who in turn repeated to Adib.

Two other sons of the sheik were there. The rest were old men, most of them endowed with good intellect but rather destitute of abstract knowledge. When they came together they engaged in the kind of warm conversation men enjoy who were suckled in common, who experienced their stages of life together, and had delicate friendships with age. Their interests were far from fatuous about Allah's blessings in their bleak surroundings. There were no variant souls among them. All tribesmen's troubles were their troubles. One slight or injury to a Bedouin brethren could not go unavenged.

"Have you been to Amman?" I asked Mohammed Ali.

He thought a moment before replying, then answered, "Yes, but it is now forbidden to travel there."

"Aqaba?"

"Yes."

"Damascus?"

"When I was a child. My father is from Syria."

"Had his family become separated?"

"Our tribe always moves together. We are never apart."

"It is my dream to see Damascus."

"Why?"

"Curiosity. Also it is perhaps the last great city of the Middle East to hold its traditions and has not become vulgarized. Adib has a sister living there."

Mohammed Ali nodded and smiled, Because I knew that Adib's sister lived in Damacus, I felt a change in his rapport, from politeness to friendliness. He said something to Adib who then said to me, "You are truly my brother, he believes. He knows we do not speak of our family to strangers."

Then Mohammed Ali began to speak directly to Avigdor in Hebrew. He had been, he said with no bitterness, two years in university, meaning an Israeli jail, for illegally crossing the frontier to Jordan. In jail he developed his Hebrew until it was nearly as easy for him as Arabic. His father had been in prison under the British. This confession was repeated for the listeners resulting in laughter and general loosening of reserve among them. Could I understand British? When I said that it was the same language as mine, the Sheik was surprised. Then he told the others, causing a discussion among the tribesmen.

Avigdor explained, comparing the New World's separation from England with the Jew's exodus from Egypt. In this way they imperfectly formed a vague picture of my origin. Their own origin was not so vague. We were soon to hear the story of how the Bedu came into being.

The sheik was a gracious man, simpler than his son, and venerated by his subjects as are most leaders the prophet sends to the faithful. Bedouin sheiks have a mysticism about them. By their mere being they possess the capacity to enhance life. They govern by the goodness of routine, for routine is law, with everything done in accordance with tradition. Desert nomads are not men of ideas, but people who thrive by timeless methods accepted by everyone. They believe or disbelieve and there is little shading between.

The tent front was wide open. No wind stirred in the brilliant afternoon. To look beyond the shade smarted the eye. The heat struck everything moving and uncovered. Men stepped inside carefully, blind for some moments before they chose where to sit. We were famished from the long drive. Even the heat had not diminished our hunger.

Now we set to it. The women brought in hot couscous heaped in such quantity on a giant tray that three strong boys were needed to carry it to the center of our circle. It was agreeably piquant and crowded with vegetables and cuts of roast lamb. The tray was twice emptied and refilled. Like Beduion hosts we were slaves to our appetites, gluttons for meat, drunkards for coffee, tea and water.

Mohammed Ali's uncle was the camp wit. Tales from him on such a day entertained our minds and eased our stomachs. He pretended not to know we were strangers and squatted before us to tell us seriously, *"It is said that in the beginning of the world there was nothing but a strong wind, that God caught a gust, spun a whirlwind and shaped man.*

"Some say instead, that our God was the wind and that from his force there trailed a man. And this man was so lonely he ran through the desert to find somebody like him, his force creating smaller winds that formed smaller men. When God went away to shape other worlds these men roasted pork, drank wine, and did evil with one another. For two centuries they fouled the earth. God returned and cut them off, leaving no record of them. Many worlds God created. And for a thousand years man was lonely. Animals had mates, and man had none.

"It is not known whether a ray of sun or the moon's light created the Prophet Allah. God asked our Prophet if he should make another universe. Prophet Allah answered that worlds without people are like goats without milk. God

was curious about this and so gave Allah the law to guard the living partner to man he would create.

"Now there are some who believe that Allah passed water to moisten the earth, then used the mud to fashion woman.

"Others know how Allah urinated in the wadi and from his stream thirty-three women emerged. With each one he lay and to each third a son was born. God was so pleased that he gave every man a grain of dust, some wind, a jug of sweet water and warmth from the sun. When they made toilet the land teemed with animals nourished from their waste. With these gifts man thrived."

Uncle was a droll clown. To denote the first wind of the world he pantomimed Bedu Kadis in judgment, bread and grain sputtering from his mouth. Being old and pudgy he looked not unlike most sheiks, who were by no means sacrosanct to him.

The tale spinner did not pass his water before us as he claimed Allah did. Even in jest he would not insult our presence. I had a moment of doubt when he moved to the center of the carpet to squat. I was half afraid a stain would be left when he moved away. What he did was somersault and roll around suggesting the play of a woman receiving the prophet Allah. What enjoyment! what hilarity!

We were not yet relaxed after his performance when mint tea was brought with honeyed cakes.

"We know our true origin, of course," the Sheik told his people, "The prophet of wisdom was formed from the dust of Mecca. The angels Gabriel and Michael were commanded to spread Mecca's sands of color, white, black and copper-red over the known world. We Bedouins of all colors, strangers to no land, are the only true believers on the known earth."

Sheik Ali asked his uncle how the infidel came into being. The answer was the shortest and wittiest of all his poetical effusions.

"They result from Mohammed's first camel."

"How the camel - from its spittle?"

Uncle shook his head.

"From its mating with the reem?"

"No."

"How then, old uncle, how?"

"The same as man," rising and shuffling to the tent opening. "The same as man, with a strong wind created by the camel of Mohammed." Saying this he extracted a noisy burb from beneath his robe while rotating his rear end outward for the coarse fragrance to carry across the hot earth.

Later we rested in a smaller tent on carpets and cushions until evening. Avigdor and I were alone while Adib conferred with the Sheik's sons and elder tribesmen. I was nearly asleep when Adib returned to inform us the group had decided that because Avigdor was a Jew he could not go with them. An excursion over the border of Jordan was planned. Adib told us they were after samples of the newly-built Amman to Aqaba roadbed. Israel military intelligence assigned this task to the tribe, a paid clandestine mission to learn if the road could support tanks and heavy equipment.

A band of Jordan Bedouins was to meet with them near *El Hufeira* just over the unmarked frontier. What exchange was offered for their part I did not know. But I later learned the other motive they had for the night crossing.

Before sun-up we were over the border, Mohammed Ali, his two brothers, Adib, myself and armed Beduions riding jeeps before and behind us. I was dressed in a brown abba with a frayed burnous to cover most of my face. The abba was gathered at my waist by a leather belt holding a crescent-shaped dagger. My face, hands and feet were darkened and brown sunglasses concealed my blue eyes. Adib cautioned me not to speak with the tribesmen we would meet.

A guide neary sixty led us, calm, quiet in comportment, with soft brown eyes. I envied those eyes. Mine were so pale in contrast, gray-blue, specked with light flecs; eyes not accustomed to the melancholy of dried spaces and limitless horizons.

Inside Jordan our numbers increased when we dismounted. Silent Arabs slipped into our file during a lenghty hike along a rocky trail overlooking a wide expanse of glittering flatlands through which ran the invisible Jordan-Israel border.

I got a good fright on the path. A dark Arab came out of the niche in which he was posted, not two yards from my left hand. He looked at me and faded back into the stone.

In the cave my presence was not questioned. I was there because Adib had declared me his brother. It was enough. Their confidence in him was trust for me. We stayed in the cave the entire day, Adib and I, with Jordan Bedouins guarding us. Those fit men from strong bands living away from population centers are a different type. Unused to formal governance true nomads have assets of mobility, toughness, intelligence and courage unseen out of their domain.

At dusk Mohammed Ali and his men returned. We left Jordan within the hour. Arabs in jeeps slipped away until we were in Negev territory with only two jeeps. Three small figures were crowded in the second jeep, silent as sheep, never looking at me when we stopped to rest. After arrival at the Bedouin camp where we had started out, and where we picked up Avigdor for our ride back to Beersheba, I learned the other motive for the illegal border crossing. Adib told us that they were girls kidnapped to replace women of the tribe who had died. Bedouin women who die are buried at night in the sands.

Replacements are either bought or stolen, depending on a tribe's ability to buy or kidnap them.

That was an exciting, not particularly risky event, but the cost was later to prove dear.

Studio

Guilat Rosen's home and studio were in a smaller damaged Arab house a few hundred yards down the hill from Avigdor's. It was between the French convent, Dames de Sion, and the Spanish Church of the Nativity of Saint John. Guilat did more ceramic work than stone sculpture, leaving those skills to Avigdor. Sarai was pleased when they teamed up because it encouraged Avigdor to create again.

Avigdor was staying there with Guilat rather than at his own home. When I visited once, she was cool toward me and I did not stay long then . Leaving her studio, I turned off the path to avoid Avigdor who was coming from his place. Sarai was not home so I hiked to Jerusalem and took the next bus to Beersheba.

A note on my bed from Yael told me that she would be looking after her mother that weekend in Herzlia.

Although I was still on Spoon River's payroll my duties were complete. The Israel Dead Sea Works was testing the operating systems of the new plant, preparing to take it over.

When I went down to the work site for a final paycheck there was a message from Sarai for me to phone her at a Tel Aviv number. I called and she agreed to meet me at noon the next day in the Jerusalem bus station..

I left a note for Yael that I would return to clear out my rooms before Wednesday next and we could discuss our future in Israel. We would decide where to live when she was given a teaching post. We would most likely to go to Cyprus to marry when her first school holiday permitted. The delay was unavoidable. She would not get an exit permit to leave Israel until she was established as a teacher. Her army service was only excused due to her studies. She would need army approval and a viable teaching contract before obtaining exit papers to visit outside Israel. We were reconciled to waiting.

I still had the key to Avigdor's room in his uncle's hotel and decided to spend a few days there after meeting with Sarai. Her bus from Tel Aviv arrived shortly after mine. We went to the hotel and though we embraced warmly, we sensed that nothing more would happen between us.

She looked well but was worried about Avigdor, and afraid for Guilat. "Guilat is good for Avigdor because he works with her, not so good when she gets into drinking bouts with him. And her sexual demands are pretty weird, even for Avigdor."

"How do you know about that?"

"Avigdor tells me everything, then when I am with Guilat she tells me."

"Tells you what?"

"Behavior you should not want to know. It's not the

loving things we used to do."

"Not much would surprise me about your husband, but maybe you're right. Perhaps I should not know."

"Guilat is terribly distraught. Last week an old lover of hers tried to force his way into her studio while Avigdor was there. Avigdor chased the guy through the garden and gashed his head when he tripped over his own sculpture. Guilat came to get me. When we tried to bandage his head Avigdor was cursing Guilat, raving that she was a raping bitch, a pig, and anything he could think of to hurt her. I held him like a naughty child, talking to him, trying to convince him that Guilat was a special friend to both of us, and that kind of friendship counts."

Sarai got up and went to the window overlooking the Orthodox Mia Sharim Quarter. Her tone was angry when she came back. "Counts for what, my husband screamed at me. Then the damn fool smashed the scale model for their project that the Arts Council had granted them. The commission was going to earn them a lot of money and rekindle their reputation."

"What can I do to help — go reason with him, take him on a trip to Greece or Paris for a month?"

"I don't know, Mac, I don'tknow."

Sarau cried while I comforted her, and soon fell asleep in my arms. I carefully lay her down and went out to get some food and wine. In half an hour I was back. Sarai came out of the shower room wearing the same Bedouin robe that Yael had worn the last time I was there with her..

"I know whose room this is," Sarai said,"it's Avigdor's."

"Yes, it is. He asked me not to tell you."

"Fools, both of you. I have always known. His uncle used to bring me here."

What she admitted somehow did not surprise me. We drank some wine and ate the sandwiches I bought.

Sarai remarked that my thoughts seemed far away.

"No," I lied.

"A love scoundrel like you can never hide your feelings."

"Yeah, my thoughts do take off sometimes but...."

"But nothing. Today I feel the intrusion more than usual."

"It's not a conscious thing."

"You must leave her back there with the Greeks."

"Yael?"

"The American, Nancy. She still crowds your heart."

I was truly surprised about Sarai's observation. Why did I show an anxiety about Nancy? Was that what caused the concern I smetimes saw in Yael's expression?

I accompanied Sarai to the bus stop, promising that I would go there to see Avigdor the next week.

Walking back to the hotel a premonition that Sarai and I might never meet again troubled me.

Little jesus boy

Riding back to Beersheba the next morning I could not unravel the kaleidoscope of anxieties searing my soul. Beersheba was unbearably hot. I took a cold shower, ate a light lunch and began discarding what I would not need when moving. Despite the heat I had to close my door and windows. A fine sand was sifting through every crack — presage to a *khamsim*.

I did not hear steps approach before rapid knocks at my door startled me. A sweaty man handed me a registered letter, said something in Hebrew, pointing to where I should sign, looked at me as if trying to fix my face in his mind, then turned and walked away through the garden to the back street. It was an official notice of some kind with my name, passport number and various dates marked between sentences which I could not make out. I put it aside for Yael to interpret when next we met.

I was not sure if she was at home in Herzylia or still doing student teaching because we had not been together for a fortnight,

I was napping around dusk when I heard my door close. Opening my eyes I saw Yael standing there, a mixed expression of concern and pleasure on her face

"I felt that you needed me today."

"Come again?"

"Or it came over me to need you very much."

"You passed your exams!" I exclaimed.

"Easily. The subjects covered exactly what I studied."

"Thank goodness you've come. I got this official looking notice that I need you to read."

She took it from the table, read it, turned it over to check the stamp and department issuing it. "I know already."

"Know what?"

"Two agents from the security branch have questioned me about you. What does it mean? What else have you done?"

"What does the notice say?"

"A declaration that your stay in Israel ends this month and that you must quit the country."

"Not possible!"

"They mean it. I know about your illegal excursion."

"The agents know too?"

"Of course they do. They have a file on every visitor in the country and every Arab within our borders."

"How did you know that I went over the border?"

"It was Adib who told me. He was questioned too, and they had named both you and Avigdor being with him during the illegal crossing. He made a special trip one night to have me warn you."

"Why did he not come to tell me that?"

"He was sure you were being watched. And you are. There are men in an auto just up the street watching this house right now."

"They are ridiculous. My work record is known. I am a friend of this country."

"They take no chances. I talked to my sister's husband who is a reserve officer in army intelligence. He said that you did a foolish thing. Intelligence knows that you worked in Sodom without a permit, but because it was for an Israeli project you were tolerated. He said that if you were other than American they would have jailed you. An illegal border crossing can be a two-year prison penalty."

"The government was part of it. It was their project. I just went for the adventure."

"It doesn't matter. Should you reveal your escapade to foreign newspapers it would make them look foolish. The government would admit nothing."

"Okay Yael, now that you know the worst, what can we do?"

An expression of exasperation swept over her features, even a shade of fear. She passed her tongue over her parched lips, absently drinking the glass of water I offered, her eyes on some far point trying to bring something out of the void for the mind to register and act on. "You are too much in my life to be sent away from me like this."

"I have no intention of going off. I'll go to my embassy. I will not leave because of this threat. I'll fight it."

"No," she said, taking my hand. "It could involve me if you make a public issue of this."

"You are coming with me."

"Not now. I cannot."

"Why not now?"

"I have to complete my treacher training contract which includes a year of service for the State. That exempts me from army service. And I must pay my family's debt to the Jewish Agency who gave us the money to come here to live. Israel would never issue me an exit visa."

"Your citizenship is French!"

"I hold dual nationality. Getting out of the country is the block. Away from Israel I travel as a French national."

"We can have you smuggled out. I have a thousand dollars saved from my work. We can get back some of the dowry money your father took. It should be enough to bribe your passage out."

"He will not give it, I know him. I had a terrible fight with my mother over that. She takes his side. I will pay you back when I begin teaching."

"Forget him then."

"Illegal departure is out of the question. The stress would be too much for me and...."

"Forgive me for saying this Yael, but I sense there is something you are shielding. Do you want me to go?"

"No, *mon cher*, I truly love you. And yes there is something else." She motioned for me sit at the edge of the bed, reaching to take my hands and pull my arms behind her waist till my head touched her body. Her voice was precise. "Rest you head against me." Turning my head so that my cheek and ear pressed against her stomach, she asked, "Do you feel anything?"

"No."

"No?"

"No."

"I want him to be born in France."

"Him?"

"My dear husband in flesh and spirit, we are going to have a child."

I held her off gently to see if her stomach had changed form, then looked up at her face with what must have been an incredulous and stupid look. Yael smiled, then the shape of her mouth changed and she cried. I cradled her in my arms for some time.

Using my shirt end to wipe her face, Yael stood in front of me, her hands on my shoulders and said firmly, "Here is my plan. I have applied to teach at a kibbutz up north for two reasons. First my father must not find me. He may kill the child if he learns about this because we didn't marry. I did not tell you before, but my mother believes in the ancient custom of killing the first born girl-child as was done before Abraham. There was a first girl-child born before she married my father. I never learned what happened to her. My two brothers and sister were born before me. I am afraid she might become deranged about my condition because are not married.

"Here is my plan; first teach up north and tell no one but my sister where I will live. Second, when Adib came to warn me we talked about what to do if you should be sent out of the country. I told him about my pregnancy. I hope you don't mind. His sister will care for our son whle he finds a way for us to leave Israel through the Druse villages to

Lebanon."

"Son?"

"I am sure it will be a son. Adib's father has two brothers living in Lebanon. Adib's sister will take him after the birth. When I am sure we are not watched, my sister and I will go with Adib's family to cross the border through mountain trails used by Druse who go back and forth without detection. If I am watched and cannot risk it, Adib and his sister will take our son to Beirut. I will come join you later somehow."

"If Adib knows a way through the north to Lebanon we will go together now."

"Not possible because you are being watched, and they will keep on watching until you have left Israel. Adib's family will get into serious trouble if you try to contact him. Should we act with haste all is lost. In this country it is the mother who determines a child's race. For them he will be a Jew, a future soldier for them."

"He? It could be a girl."

"It will be a boy."

"All right Yael, he will be our son."

"I must appear to be a good Jewish mother or the State will take him from me. I know how they are. My sister will tell my parents we have quarreled and that you have left Israel. My father will not know why. It is enough for him to keep your money. My mother will be relieved that you are not here to take me away. We must do it my way: the birth, Adib's family to care for the baby, and teaching until I can get away, then freedom to come to you with our son."

"That can take many months, even a year to bring off."

"Please, there is no other way, believe me. Trust Adib. And trust my love. It will hold well for you here." She placed my hand on her stomach. "This is you. I will sleep, eat, pray, work and dream with you inside me."

"Yael, I do not know all the suffering your family endured in Algeria, you have said so little about your life. It has sharpened your intuition and given you a quality of volatile magic that has woven around me a confidence and love I never thought to possess. I shall go quietly, wander a bit, then settle and make a home worthy of you and the child in France, the country you love."

"Express love to me in your letters. I shall need it to sustain me here without you." She kissed me, and again read the official letter, put it down and calmly helped me pack for my leaving Beersheba.

The *khamsin* held us enclosed that Shabbath Friday and all the next day. How did we let it come about, this moment, which should have been so tender, so secure to begin the future? On the frail shoulders of this brave girl was placed the burden of my departure. With courageous determination Yael would manage this crisis. A hoarding of the genius of their women, this Jewish humility. I shall always feel the warmth of Yael's small body folded against me tender with our child.

Coming Home

Leaving Beersheba for the l;ast time I carried what I valued in two duffle bags, took the bus to Jerusalem, checked the bags in the station and went to Avigdor's hotel room to gather the few items I had there. Late that afternoon I boarded the number 10 bus to Ein Karim. Descending near the village I took the path to Guilat's house. She was in her work studio seated at the clay turntable, bare feet spinning the stone, her pudgy hands streaked with clay mud deftly shaping something.

Avigdor was sleeping off a drunk spell in Guilat's bedroom. It took a few minutes of greeting and telling her what Sarai worried about.

"I know how she feels. What do you think about us."

Shruging, I did not want to tell her nor, did I want to judge her role supplying Avigdor with alcohol and more sex than he could deal with. I could have cautioned her that Avigdor's nature threatened her status as an artist. I also could have,

Sodom and a Greek Passion

perhaps I should have told her to consider the harm to Sarai and her sons. But I said nothing. Anyway she knew, she really knew.

"He is an unlovely man. I tried to find the beauty in him, but it's not there to find. Even my naked, unfired figures have beauty. If Avigdor ever was a lovely msn, like Sarai says she remembers him, it lies rotted in his burning soul.

"You know, Guilat, you can remake a piece before it's baked, and once fired you can't expose the faults without breaking it. There are rules about duggung for defects, ways to behave with illness. "I almost pity him."

"Once you try to love him and he rejects you only pity is left. He can keep his mystery. I feed him his bottle and take what I need from him. God knows how I need him, but Avigdor doesn't give a shit about that. Sometimes he won't let me near him. Other times he wants me naked when I work. Strange isn't it, or terrible, who knows?"

"You know Guilat, you know."

"He spews malice and pain on me like pig offal. I"m fat, unfeminine, unclean. I cannot refuse whatever he wants me to do. What he does to me is far beyond normal, even for a psycho like him. I want to kill him."

"Why haven't you?"

"Because he is the only stone-master I can work with. the only partner who will get my recognition back to the level it was when we did the Ashkalon project. And he is the only man in three yeasrs who wants to fuck me. I need him. I need him." The anxiety and pain she suffered with Avigdor was what Sarai tolerated most of their married life. Guilat held up the clay object she had shaped in the form of a twisted penis and set it inside the dry kiln for the next firing.

After listening to Guilat spew out the frustration of her sordid life with Sarai's husband I could not go over to Sarai's house that night. I left Ein Karim by a back lane around Guilat's garden to the road that would lead me back to Jerusalem.

Oh my ersatz cousin, Avigdor, flawed by a limping spirituality, and mentally lost in our holistic world. Like many of us who have tasted the fruits of Eden he cannot cast out the evil madness in his guts. His soul is trapped in the bellows of an antique camera unable to focus on those who love him.

When I entered the hotel there were three agents from internal security were waiting for me. My two duffle bags from the bus station checkroom had been dumped out on the bed. They motioned for me to pack my stuff back into the bags, but I shook my head and abandoned all of it. My passport and peronal papers were handed to me when they put me in their car. Saying nothing to me I was locked up at the Tel Aviv airport police post until the next flight to New York was ready to take off.

Perdition

My son was brought to my cabin with winter's grief, grief keener than the cold river. Yael's sister, Miriam brouight him swathed against the cold like a Druse child. She told me that Yael had not been well since he was born.

"The birth was hard on my sister. Her worry that the State might take him forced Yael to ask me to help. We got your son from the hospital at night amd hid with Adib's sister near Rama. Abu Hasib guided us through the trail into Lebanon where his cousin's family sheltered us. My passport was altered to name me the mother of Francis-Guillaume, the name Yael chose for your son."

"Whare is Yael now. She has not written since I have been here?"

"She does not dare to send you a letter from Israel. She was placed on army reserve and believes that she is carefully monitored at her school. They will conscript her to the regular army if they suspect she tries to contact you, or has any dealings with Adib and his family. Whatever free time Yael has is spent with Sarai in Ein Karim.

"A mistake to have left her," I said to Miriam. "A mistake to have done the stupid thing that forced me out of her life when she needed me most. I wish that my soul was barren, that my memory would obliterate everything from my past. The visions that damage my sleep are hellish. My twisted memories are too damaging to endure."

"It is not desirable for a man to suffer all the sorrows alone that he endures in life. We women share the blame with you.?

Miriam did not look like her sister, but she did resemble Sarai physically, and possessed the same caring concern for my well-being that Sarai had. I was pleased that Miriam has spirited my son out of Israel and made the long journey to me here. Until then I was hopeful that Yael would also come to me. The disquiet about her remaining behind and the loneliness of isolation had plagued me with poverty of spirit, and the guilt of failure. The pitiless repitition of my damning behavior was patiently heard by Miriam."

"Only a sterile life leaves nothing for a man to reproach.. Yael understands that. And I do not judge you. I am here for you to be like my sister, to love the son of Yael and the father of her son like she would love you.

What I did not reveal to Miriam was, that on some nights, when I took her in the dark she bore the features of all loving women, and only one of them was her sister, Yael.

One night when I could not sleep I looked in on Francis-Guillaume and pressed my cheek on his pillow, stroked his head and placed my palm on the imprint to feel the warmth of his mother's touch. How I love this boy, this trusting soul of creative love. Life has just begun to etch the lines on the face of a new being creeping into a careless world.

Miriam stood in the doorway. She led me away like a sister taking her brother to bed.

Miriam left us for nearly a month to learn what was happening with her sister. She returned disappointed that they did not meet. She learned from Sarai that Avigdor, Yael and Adib had all made it over the border to the Druse headquarters of their leader, Jumblatt, on the outskirts of Beirut. There they would wait until the Greek sailor, Yiannis would take them aboard for the journey across the Mediterranean. She dared not risk crossing the border to search for them in Lebanon, believing that her sister would make it to America and join us here.

One brisk morning my son and I were in the woods, the boy creeping over a fallen log. I heard the postman's motorbke turning into my yard. When I got to the yard Miriam was holding an envelope from Israel. I asked her to open the letter. I watched her reading the first page, turning to the second, then back to the first, Her mouth was set in a grim line, her eyes darting from sentence to sentence, then looking up toward me. The moment she handed the letter to me, Miriam began crying. Picking up my son she carried him into the cabin. The letter, addressed to me, was written in Hebrew except for the last paragraph.

"...three weeks have gone since Adib sent word that they had crossed Lebanon to take refuge in a Druse area controlled by Druse militiamen. I was so happy for you, believing that you, your son and Yael would soon be together. The word that came from Adib's family was crushing, The Druse command house outside Beirut with all its guests did not survive an air attack by our own warplanes that destroyed the village where my husband, Adib and Yael were staying until they could leave Lebanon.
Oh unholy Moses, my husband is gone, Yael and Adib are gone. Bloody Moses, Yael is dead.

the end

Born in Chicago, July 31, 1920, Robert Waltz now lives and writes in San Francisco and Vancouver, Canada

Author of six novels, two screen plays and numerous short stories, Waltz wandered all over Europe and the Middle East in his restless years following WWII when he drove a Sherman tank with the 16th Armored Division in General Patton's Third Army in France, Germany and Czechoslovakia.

Waltz sampled four colleges on the GI Bill in England, Chicago and New York, sandwiched between marriages and babies on $110.00 a month.

In the spring of 1957 he left a job and a wife to go write in Paris for six months. The months stretched to nineteen years before touching America again.

His early books were published by the famed Olympia Press in Paris in English and French, in Dutch and French by Elsevier, Amsterdam and Brussels, and translated to Hebrew by Atid Publishers in Tel Aviv. His favorite novel published by Olympia was later purloined by Pendulum Books in Atlanta for which he was never paid royalties.

Waltz claims that he is not unduly concerned with linking his writing to sociological interpretation. He wants to portray a writers caring towards earth's creatures. *"Sociology, psychology, philosophy are better left with those trained to play with it."*

ISBN 1-55212-358-8